They passsement of quality and o pick up a green p and plop it on h nk?"

What she thought was that he was trying to cajole her out of a bad mood, and she adored his flippant nature. It was the perfect antidote to everything weighing on her.

"Not actually the best look for you." She laughed. Her gaze landed on a cowboy hat. Every true Texan needed one. "Here, try this."

Obligingly, Ty settled it on his head, then tipped it back with a finger to smile down at her.

Those blue-gray eyes hit her full force, and her breath caught. Damn, he was a good-looking man. She hadn't realized just how close they were standing until that moment, and it seemed like the most natural thing in the world to slide her hands around his waist and reach up to meet his kiss.

Dear Reader,

Thank goodness the Texas Hill Country offers calorie-burning opportunities like hiking, cycling and dancing—they're necessary to counterbalance all the fantastic food in the area! If you've ever attended the Fredericksburg Food and Wine Fest, or even just stopped for dinner in the region, you'll understand my inspiration for this book.

In my first Hill Country Heroes story *(Claimed by a Cowboy)* I briefly introduced chef Grace Torres and her family's restaurant, The Twisted Jalapeño. Now Grace is a contestant on a televised cooking competition that will be filmed during a local festival. She needs the prize money and publicity to save her restaurant. But she's about to meet her match in charmer Ty Beckett.

Ty's flirtatious banter and lazy smiles mask a steely determination. As a kid who grew up poor and hungry, he swore he'd make something of himself. Now, he's trying to negotiate a deal to host his own cooking show, and the producers have hinted that if he wins the highly publicized competition in Fredericksburg, the contract is his. Ty has never let anything stand in his way. He relishes the challenge of facing down fiery-tempered Grace. Neither expected that, on the way to winning, they might lose their hearts….

Happy reading,

Tanya

P.S. To hear about what I'm cooking up next, "like" Author Tanya Michaels on Facebook or follow TanyaMichaels on Twitter.

Tamed by a Texan

TANYA MICHAELS

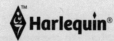

TORONTO NEW YORK LONDON
AMSTERDAM PARIS SYDNEY HAMBURG
STOCKHOLM ATHENS TOKYO MILAN MADRID
PRAGUE WARSAW BUDAPEST AUCKLAND

Recycling programs
for this product may
not exist in your area.

ISBN-13: 978-0-373-75403-8

TAMED BY A TEXAN

www.Harlequin.com

Printed in U.S.A.

ABOUT THE AUTHOR

Three-time RITA® Award nominee Tanya Michaels writes about what she knows—community, family and lasting love! Her books, praised for their poignancy and humor, have received honors such as the Booksellers' Best Bet Award, the Maggie Award of Excellence and multiple readers' choice awards. She was also a *2010 RT Book Reviews* nominee for Career Achievement in Category Romance. Tanya is an active member of Romance Writers of America and a frequent public speaker, presenting workshops to educate and encourage aspiring writers. She lives outside Atlanta with her very supportive husband, two highly imaginative children and a household of quirky pets, including a cat who thinks she's a dog and a bichon frise who thinks she's the center of the universe.

Books by Tanya Michaels

HARLEQUIN AMERICAN ROMANCE

HARLEQUIN TEMPTATION

Belated thanks to Susan Lang, who walked me through my first official wine tasting!

Chapter One

Chef Grace Torres had inherited her Irish mother's fiery nature and her late father's impressively thorough knowledge of Spanish swear words, both of which were about to boil to the surface on this gloomy February morning.

"I can't believe you two!" Grace gripped the edge of the stainless-steel workstation so she wouldn't do anything stupid, like start throwing plates. The restaurant had enough financial burdens without having to replace dishes.

Ben's and Victor's nervous expressions might have been funny under different circumstances. Both of her brothers were older than Grace—who'd been an unplanned souvenir from her parents' fifteenth-anniversary cruise—and they each stood close to six feet. Not that Ben could stand right now—he'd been injured during an arson investigation and would be in a wheelchair for another few weeks. Grace was the runt of the Torres family and claimed to be five-three, which was true when she wore heels. In height, she'd taken after her aunt, small but fierce *Tía* Maria, instead of her parents.

"Now, Graciela…" Victor was the oldest, and his tone bordered on patronizing.

Her already simmering temper began to bubble and pop.

"We know you love this place," Ben quickly interrupted, secure in the knowledge that his broken leg and still-mending ribs would keep her from smacking him upside the head with a rubber spatula. "We all love it, but—"

"Ha! You love eating here, trying out new specialties before I put them on the menu and bringing your dates to woo them with the nostalgia factor. But you don't… The two of you have never—" She broke off, eyes burning, and spun abruptly, turning her back on her brothers. *I will not cry in front of them.* It would be such a clichéd girl thing to do.

She battled the threat of tears with a stream of words that would have made her dad grin and her mother threaten to ground her from the kitchen. Colleen Torres had once said Grace was the only teenager in Texas who got more upset about losing cooking privileges than being forbidden to go to the movies with friends. Grace and her friends had rarely gone to the theater, though. They'd had movie nights at her house, where Grace prepared a menu of snacks themed to go with the rented DVDs.

"Guess I should brush up on my Spanish," Victor said behind her. "I consider myself bilingual, but I only understood half of that."

"I got all of it," Ben said. "Trust me, you're better off not knowing."

When she faced them again, Grace was calmer. "I realize you're both going through difficult times."

Ben, the lawman, was on medical leave, and Victor, who worked for a local bank, had recently separated from his wife of nine years.

"But let's not panic," she continued, "and do something we can't take back." Like sell the restaurant, her heart and soul. *My home.*

Of all the things she'd inherited from her family, The

Twisted Jalapeño was what she most cherished. The modest restaurant nestled in Texas Hill Country was a Torres legacy. It not only kept her close to the beloved father they'd lost three years ago, the Jalapeño gave her an opportunity to develop her own talent, putting her stamp on the place. She had big plans and hoped to bridge the gap between the past and a bright future for generations of Torreses to come.

Victor sighed, running a hand through his inky-black hair. All three siblings had the same dark hair and eyes. Colleen, a pale redhead with ethereal features, used to laugh at the surprise on people's faces when they realized she was their mother. "It's not only Ben and I who have hit bumps in the road," Victor pointed out gently. "You think we're so preoccupied with our problems that we don't see how hard everything's been on you? Putting in crazy hours here, breaking up with Jeff last week, the situation with Mom."

Grace winced at mention of their mother, recalling the stab of guilt when she'd gone to visit Colleen yesterday. The woman had been confused about where she was and how she'd gotten there, asking her daughter, "Are you here to take me home, Gracie?" *I hope we did the right thing.* Grace and her brothers had agonized over the decision to move their increasingly disoriented mom from her long-time home to an apartment in a supervised facility.

Instead of dwelling on that, Grace focused on the far less painful split with her boyfriend. "It was fun for a few months, but Jeff clearly doesn't understand me. He was mad I wouldn't make huge Valentine's Day plans with him because I needed to be here. He should have been more flexible! February 14 is a number on the calendar, not a test of loyalty. We could have been just as romantic together on the fifteenth."

Ben held up a hand, his expression pained. "I'm gonna stop you there. Don't really want to hear about my baby sister's romantic escapades."

"I'm twenty-six." She rolled her eyes. "Plenty old enough for…escapades."

But her grumbled words were a matter of form, not a declaration of interest in dating. Truthfully Jeff had been right about her priorities, which was why she'd kindly told him he should find someone else. Once the restaurant was back on its feet—and her brothers weren't hounding her to sell it—she could worry about romance.

"I was saving this for Sunday dinner," she said, "but since you two decided to ambush me…" She strolled out of the kitchen with no further explanation, confident they'd follow.

Grace really had been planning to share the big news with her family this weekend. Even before they'd moved Colleen into one of the assisted-care apartments, they'd gone to the complex on Sundays to have dinner with *Tía* Maria. The wizened seventy-four-year-old woman had outlived both her husband and her younger brother, Grace's father. Unlike Colleen, Maria's mind was still as sharp as her tongue had always been. She'd moved into the apartments willingly after breaking her hip one year, claiming she liked the smaller living space and the twice a week housekeeping help. Grace took some comfort in knowing Maria visited her sister-in-law every day and helped soothe Colleen when she became confused.

Inside the tiny office adjacent to the storeroom, Grace opened the bottom drawer of the scarred wooden desk and withdrew a manila envelope with her name on it. Just seeing it made her heart beat faster in a combination of exhilaration and nerves. She took a steadying breath while she waited for Ben to roll his way into the office. Victor walked behind his brother.

"This better be good," Ben said. "It's not a piece of cake to wheel down that hallway."

She shoved away her remembered horror at hearing he'd been hurt, keeping her tone light. "Oh, quit your whining. Wheeling yourself around is probably good for your upper body strength." She waved the envelope. "Behold, the next step in my plan to revitalize the restaurant."

Ben widened his eyes in a comical attempt at fear. "We're still trying to adjust to your last step. You know she has people drinking something called a blueberry tequila sour?"

A couple of months ago, Grace had hired Amy Winthrop, a mixologist from Austin who'd been adding signature twists to traditional cocktails. Some of the regulars had been shy about trying her more outlandish margarita flavors, but Amy was slowly winning them over, just as Grace was gradually winning fans with her fusion dishes. The restaurant still served some of the classics that had been on the menu since her grandparents first opened the doors, but there were a thousand places from here to the border where a person could order a burrito. Grace wanted the Jalapeño to stand out.

And my brothers want to sell it. The three of them owned it jointly, which meant Ben and Vic held the majority vote. She had to convince them she could do this.

Her gaze swiveled from Ben in his chair to Victor in his suit and tie. "I realize you guys watch ESPN and that Wall Street show, not Food Network, but even if you've never seen them, you have to know there are a lot of cooking shows on the air. There's a new one called *Road Trip* that focuses on different regions of the country, hosting multiepisode competitions in each location. In March, they're spotlighting the Texas Hill Country Food and Wine Association and filming challenges at Frederick-Fest." The ten-day annual festival was always a major draw for both tourists and culinary professionals.

"And guess who made it through the selection process and is one of the semifinalists!" Despite her best efforts to demonstrate businesslike competence, her voice squeaked with excitement.

"They picked you?" Victor asked.

"Of course they did." Ben winked at her. "They'd be fools not to! Way to go, hermanita."

She beamed. "Thank you."

Victor was not as caught up in his siblings' enthusiasm. "I assume this televised competition is going to take a lot of your time next month. How are we going to keep the restaurant running smoothly? In a perfect world, Ben and I would cover it, but he'll be on crutches. And I have a full-time job at the bank, not to mention meetings with lawyers and trying to schedule time with my own children."

"Plus," Ben inserted, "neither of us can cook."

Victor ducked his head. "That, too."

"Temporarily we can cancel the lunch shift and open only for dinner. Plenty of places around here do that," she added in a rush. "It wouldn't be forever, just long enough for us to snag all the free publicity the competition will bring. One of the judges is an editor whose food magazine will do write-ups on the contestants and the show's website will run streaming videos of cooking demonstrations and other footage. This will be great for us!"

"I don't know how I feel about you pinning all your hopes on this," Victor said slowly. Ever since the woman he'd planned to be with till death parted them had told him they were no longer compatible, he'd been a lot more pessimistic. To be fair, though, as the person who kept the books for the Jalapeño, he knew better than anyone that they were barely scraping along. "You could work for someone else, Grace, and have all the joy of cooking without the responsibility of everything else. We didn't suggest selling the place because we don't believe in you."

"I don't want to sell," she said mulishly.

"I miss Dad, too." Victor's voice started to rise. "But sinking all our time and money into this old restaurant won't bring him back!"

She flinched, too stung to form a response.

"Whoa," Ben interjected. "Let's everyone take a second. Getting a little tense in here."

Lowering her gaze and her voice, Grace said, "I need this. I can win!"

Just as softly, Victor rebutted, "You don't know that. No one's disputing your talent, but competition is like owning a restaurant. There's a lot of luck involved and timing and—"

"If I lose, you can sell the restaurant." Grace hadn't known she was going to say the words until she heard them. But rather than add to her anxiety, the impulsive promise wrapped around her like a soothing hug. *I can do this.*

Once again, Ben and Victor exchanged glances, an entire conversation passing between them with nothing said. Finally Victor nodded.

"All right, you have a deal." He paused, holding her gaze a long moment before adding, "Good luck."

SUNLIGHT RIPPLED ACROSS the surface of the water. Not a single cloud marred the expanse of blue overhead. Country music piped through discreet poolside speakers, accompanied by the melodic rush of a small landscaped waterfall that ran over natural-looking rocks. The shirtless man drifting lazily on an inflated lounge chair grinned. It was a damn good day to be Ty Beckett.

"But then," he drawled aloud, "every day is a good day to be me."

From the nearby patio table came a grunt. "Don't get too comfy," his business manager cautioned without looking away from his laptop. "We have to clear out soon. You have an interview with an entertainment reporter from the *Statesman* at three-thirty and that restaurant opening tonight."

"Too bad we couldn't invite the reporter here to Cody's place and do the interview in the pool. Did you see the picture with her byline? Bet she looks smokin' in a bikini." At his manager's reproachful silence, Ty added, "I'm just sayin'."

Ty sighed. "You are no fun, dude. Not that you ever were, but you're even less so lately."

Stephen Zigler glared over top of his sunglasses. "You mean now that I'm married and have a baby on the way and generally choose to act like an adult? I swear, if Donna wasn't plagued by round-the-clock cravings for that secret-recipe potato salad of yours, I'd drop you as a client."

"When we're on the verge of hitting it big? No, you wouldn't." Ty stuck his hand into the water and paddled toward the steps. Despite the bright sun, the early-March temperature would be too brisk for swimming if the pool weren't temperature-regulated. He climbed the stairs, glancing around at the sculpted yard and Cody Black's million-dollar Barton Creek mansion. "Someday I'll have a place like this."

Stephen turned, his expression startled. "You sound serious."

"I am."

"Yeah, but…it's *you*. Sounding serious. I didn't think you knew what the word meant."

Ty ignored the gibe. Despite Ty's devil-may-care persona, his manager knew better than anyone how hard the celebrity chef worked. *Well, not a full-fledged celebrity yet.* But he was definitely on the right path. Last night, for instance, he'd been hired to cook for the three dozen closest friends of country music star Cody Black, who'd wanted to celebrate his fortieth birthday with an "intimate" dinner. As her gift, Cody's wife had booked them a European vacation before his next tour started; they'd left this morning. Cody had invited Ty to stick around for a few hours and enjoy the pool and high-tech game room.

Nathan Tyler Beckett, the skinny kid who'd grown up in a series of south Texas trailer parks, wouldn't have even believed a house like this existed.

"I'm gonna grab a shower," Ty said, "and make sure all my stuff's packed up from the kitchen. Then we'll hit the road."

Two hours later, Ty sat in an upscale Austin restaurant while a beautiful blonde smiled across the table. As much as he enjoyed looking at her, her questions were all ones he'd heard before. His mind kept wandering from the mundane conversation to the appetizer sampler they'd ordered. The fried pickles tasted too much like the inside of a deep fryer and whoever was responsible for the bland travesty of aioli should be shot. Other offerings were intriguing, though. He was trying to dissect the ingredients of the house Loco Guacamole, which included not only pumpkin but—

"I'm sure my readers will be interested to know, how'd

you get hooked on cooking in the first place?" the blonde asked.

He flashed her a practiced smile. "Would it make me sound desperate if I said I started cooking because I wanted to impress women?"

Her cheeks turned a rosy-pink. "I don't think anyone could ever mistake you for desperate, Chef Beckett."

"Ty. Please." He widened his grin. "It all began back in middle school with Family and Consumer Sciences, which was their fancy name for what used to be called Home Ec."

There were grains of truth in his stock answer. He had, after all, taken Family and Consumer Sciences, which included a cooking component. But Ty hadn't been there for the cute female students. He'd wanted the free food each lesson brought, supplementing the state-funded school lunches he qualified for because of his family's poverty level. By the time Ty was thirteen, he'd been growing like a weed and constantly hungry. Beth, his single mother, had never been able to put much on the table. During his teen years, there had been times late at night or even in the middle of class when he'd catch himself fantasizing about food with the same intensity other guys his age probably daydreamed of cheerleaders.

But he didn't share those memories with anyone. Ever.

"So what's next for you?" the reporter asked. "I know you've traveled extensively, helping new restaurants find their feet and developing menu items before you move on to the next challenge. Some of us wonder, will Chef Ty Beckett ever settle down?"

Not until the price was right. He'd followed specific strategic opportunities, constantly building on his name and reputation, rather than investing in a place of his own.

"You never know," he said enigmatically. "But as for

what's next, I'm one of the ten semifinalists in a cooking competition that will be filmed in Fredericksburg this month. Fans will have to watch the show to see how I do, but I can tell you right now, I plan to win."

A cable network had hinted this show was his informal audition. Ty had done televised segments before and was popular with audiences. Male viewers liked him because he eschewed fancy French terms they were suspicious of and offered grilling advice real men could use; women loved him because… Well, women just loved him. If Ty won this Frederick-Fest competition, getting his own show was a done deal. He could be a household name one day like other famous chefs before him.

And being a household name paid well.

His companion leaned back against her side of the booth, looking impressed. "Your skills *are* legendary," she conceded, looking him up and down in such a way that made him wonder just which skills she meant. "But I'm sure the other nine chefs are very talented, too. You believe you'll beat them?"

Ty gave a decisive nod. "Bet on it."

Chapter Two

"Can't sleep?" Amy Winthrop stood at the edge of the kitchen wearing an oversize University of Texas Longhorns jersey that fell almost to her knees.

Grace looked up guiltily from the batter she'd been stirring. "Sorry. Didn't mean to wake you." Maybe middle of the night cupcake experimentation hadn't been such a good idea.

Her roommate waved a dismissive hand. "It wasn't you. I've screwed up my sleep cycle for all eternity. The job I had before this, I rarely got home before five in the morning. A bunch of us would clean up the bar after closing, then go for breakfast at one of those twenty-four-hour diners. I'm trying to retrain myself to be normal."

Grace grinned at the woman's eggplant-purple hair, which clashed spectacularly with her burnt-orange shirt, and sparkling eyebrow ring. A row of small hoop earrings curled up her left ear. "*Re*train? That implies there was a time when you were normal."

Amy grabbed a dish towel off the counter, wadded it and threw it at Grace, who laughed.

The two of them had hit it off within minutes of meeting each other last fall. Grace had been in Austin for the weekend and ordered one of Amy's drinks, which had been exceptional. They'd talked on and off all night as

Amy served other patrons. Before Grace left, she'd impulsively pulled out a business card for The Twisted Jalapeño. "You ever want to relocate to Fredericksburg, you have a job waiting for you."

Still, Grace had been shocked when Amy walked into the restaurant six weeks later. Amy and her fiancé had called it quits and she needed a change of pace. Meanwhile, Grace, who'd been living with her mom at the time, had agreed with Ben and Victor that it was time to sell the house to help pay for Colleen to have professional care. Grace and Amy had decided to pool their limited resources, and they'd moved into the small two-bedroom carriage-house apartment behind the Henderson family. There wasn't much space, but it was a cute place and Grace enjoyed the company. After growing up with brothers, she looked at Amy as the sister she'd never had.

"You sure you want to start with me?" Grace picked up the towel that had just missed her and brandished it with deadpan menace. "I'm *muy peligrosa.*"

"Dangerous? You?" Amy snorted. "Bring it on, shorty."

Although Amy was at least two inches taller than Grace, the bartender had a very delicate build. A strong breeze might knock her over. Grace, while short, was curvy. *Nothing delicate about me.* She was all right with that. Who would trust a chef who looked like a twig? Besides, the guys she'd dated had told her she was rounded in all the best places.

Amy pulled down a glass and filled it with water. "So what's with the late-night cooking spree? Sudden inspiration for a new dessert menu?"

"Nerves," Grave admitted. "About tomorrow night." Or, more accurately, she realized with a glance at the clock, *tonight.*

"But the competition doesn't even begin until Monday.

Tomorrow, you're just being introduced to some judges and the other contestants." One of the local vineyards was hosting a reception, an opening ceremony of sorts.

"And you don't think spending the evening with a bunch of people who are going to shape my future is nerve-racking? I, uh, got the list today," she admitted. She hadn't told anyone because she'd had this weird superstitious response to seeing the other names, as if talking about the impressive chefs on the list somehow added to their power.

Two vertical lines appeared over Amy's nose as her forehead puckered in a frown. "What list? I'm not following."

"When I was first notified I'd made it through the selection process," Grace backtracked, "I was told I was one of ten chefs, but I didn't think I'd know who the others were until we got started. Today they emailed me a list." She'd printed it out along with some final paperwork she had to sign.

"And you're just now telling me?" Amy demanded. "Gimme names, woman!"

Grace sighed, abandoning the cupcake batter. She crossed the kitchen to the slotted wooden box on the wall where they kept mail and bills. She wasn't sure why she retrieved the message and unfolded it—she'd already memorized the other nine names. Hoping Amy wouldn't interrupt to *ooh* and *aah* over the combined talent, she sped through the list. There were men and women of varying ages and specialties, from all over Texas. Katharine Garner currently worked as an executive chef in New York but had grown up in Dallas; Grace wasn't sure where Texas-born Ty Beckett lived. He seemed to bounce all over the place.

"Ty Beckett?" Amy fluttered her eyelashes. "I saw him

at a couple of events in Austin. Do you have any idea how hot he is?"

"He's not *that* good-looking," Grace grumbled. "I've seen him on TV."

"Okay, one." Amy jabbed an index finger in her friend's direction. "You are a lousy liar. No talent for it whatsoever, so don't bother trying. And, two, take it from me, he's even better looking in person."

"That's probably why they selected him," Grace said, trying to bolster herself. "He's so photogenic. He'll look good on television."

"Also, he's supposed to be a phenomenal chef."

Grace groaned. "Whose side are you on? I'm sure he's very good, but I can beat him, right? He has little formal training that I've heard of, doesn't have a restaurant of his own and his entire career seems to consist of flitting from one thing to the next. Do you think he loses focus, gets bored easily?" That could bode well for his competitors. Serious cooking required lots of patience.

Her pride niggled at her. Didn't she want to be named the best because of how hard she'd worked at her craft? Would it be as satisfying to beat Ty Beckett because he got distracted by something shiny or bailed midway through the competition? Then again, if the end result was that she got to keep her restaurant...

"I don't know," Amy said. "I realize that in the media he seems very flirty and like he doesn't take anything seriously, but, to the best of my knowledge, he hasn't lost any culinary competition in *years*. Don't let his attitude fool you. He may crack jokes and not look like he's exerting much effort, but my gut tells me, when Ty Beckett wants something, he goes for it."

"Yeah?" Grace raised an eyebrow. "Well, so do I."

"REMIND ME AGAIN WHY WE'RE stopping here for dinner when we're on our way to a party with lots of food," Stephen said from the passenger seat. "While you're at it, remind me how it is that you ended up driving my car."

Ty flashed a grin. "Because people find it impossible to tell me no. And we're here because there was only one person on that list neither of us know anything about, and coincidentally, she happens to be local. Or maybe not coincidentally. Do you think they picked her to keep the Hill Country sponsors happy?"

"As opposed to any of the other dozens of award-winning Hill Country chefs and restaurateurs?" Stephen said wryly. "Face it, if she's in the game, she's probably something special."

"Must be." Ty peered into the darkness surrounding them. "Because, hard as this place is to find, they'd need incredible word of mouth to stay in business. Haven't these people heard of neon signs?" There were a couple of parking lights shining down on the pothole-riddled lot, but nothing lit up with the name of the place. According to the one-line bio in the paperwork Stephen had received, her restaurant was The Twisted Jalapeño.

He parked the car. "We're not really eating dinner, you know. Just order something small and I'll do the same, so we can get a feel for the place. The reception doesn't start until seven. We have time."

"Assuming we don't get lost again," Stephen said. His phone was equipped with a GPS navigational system, but based on their experience trying to get Ty to his hotel this afternoon, the GPS was a compulsive liar.

"We're not going to get lost," Ty said as they crunched across the gravel lot. "In a couple of hours, we'll meet the people who are going to help me get my own show. This is it, my big break. Trust the Beckett Instinct. When have I ever steered you wrong? And before you make some wise-ass comment, I'd like to remind you who introduced you to your wife."

"Caroline Groves introduced me to my wife, you lunatic. You weren't even there."

"Yeah, but if I hadn't been ducking Caroline's calls, she wouldn't have cornered you at that museum benefit, which led to you meeting Donna. So I claim credit." Ty opened the restaurant door and stepped inside.

Music played merrily overhead, and Ty quirked an eyebrow. If he wasn't mistaken, that was an Irish reel. Not exactly what he'd expected.

A smiling hostess with a profusion of curly hair greeted them. "Two this evening, gentlemen?"

"Yes, ma'am. But we can't stay long," Ty said apologetically. "So no need to waste a table on us. Seats at the bar would be fine."

"You got it." She gestured toward the back corner of the room. "Amy's got some great specials going on tonight. Enjoy."

The decor consisted mostly of framed photographs. Old black-and-white family pictures intermingled with colorful landscapes of the region. He recognized shots of Main Street from his exploring town this afternoon. There was a photo of three kids, a tiny dark-haired girl standing between two lanky boys, in front of The Twisted Jalapeño. He wondered how long the restaurant had been doing business. The place had its charm—and something certainly smelled good—but as he and Stephen walked through the dining area, he noted signs of age and disrepair. This restaurant needed some TLC...if "TLC" stood for infusion of cash.

About half the tables they passed were occupied, but the bar was mostly empty. At one end, a woman spoke into her cell phone while twirling a straw in her margarita; at the other was a man in a suit, with a laptop in front of him. Ty and Stephen took seats at the middle of the counter. The bartender had purple hair and a butterfly tattoo on her upper arm, revealed by her blue tank top and black leather vest.

She smiled at them. "Can I interest you two in…" She trailed off, blinking at Ty, then mumbled something.

He couldn't be one hundred percent sure, but he *thought* she said, "Oh, this should be good."

She walked away briefly, returning with a basket of tortilla chips and some green salsa. "Those are our drink specials tonight." She pointed to a chalkboard at the end of the bar. "And here are a couple of menus. Be back in a minute to take your order."

Before either man had a chance to speak, she hustled to the far end of the bar, to the man in the suit. They had a quick conversation in low voices. Ty didn't betray his curiosity by looking toward them. Instead he swiped a chip through the salsa and nodded.

"Excellent," he pronounced.

He flipped open the menu and was studying the range of selections when he sensed motion. Ty glanced over his shoulder. A woman in a formfitting green dress was stalking toward him, her long black hair bouncing against her shoulders. She was one of those women for whom the expression "you're beautiful when you're angry" had been created, although Ty had no idea why she looked so ticked.

"Incoming," he said under his breath to Stephen.

Stephen took a quick look, then shook his head. "Tell me you didn't date her and break her heart. There must be a hundred females in the world who want you dead."

"Not true," Ty objected. The benefit of keeping his relationships casual was that women tended not to be heart-broken when he left. Most of his breakups were amicable, including the food critic who'd given him a glowing write-up even after they stopped seeing each other. "Besides, you know me, I'm a pain in the ass. By the time I leave, they're relieved to see me go."

"You!" The woman had reached them. Her narrowed eyes were sharper than the best set of knives he'd ever owned. "You have a lot of nerve."

Ty gave her a disarming smile. "It's true, ma'am. I've always had more nerve than brains. Have we met? Ty Beckett."

"Oh, I know who you are, Mr. Beckett. You're the competition and you've come to spy."

"Spy? Ah. You must be Grace Torres," he deduced. "Look, it isn't as if I came in here to steal your recipes. Although, kudos on this salsa verde. It would definitely be worth stealing." He waited a beat to see if the compliment improved her opinion of him. *Nope.* "I was just stopping by on my way to the reception because I was intrigued. You were a mystery. I've heard of all the other finalists."

When Stephen coughed, choking on his chip, Ty realized his phrasing might not have been the best way to break the ice, insinuating she was a nobody in the culinary world.

To cover his uncharacteristic gaffe, Ty offered quickly, "Hey, we could all ride together. Want a lift to the vineyard?"

Grace drew back, her almond-shaped eyes incredulous. "I'd rather walk."

"In those heels?" Ty teased. "Might be uncomfortable." He'd noticed the shoes because they were sexy as hell and did great things for her exposed calves, but he kept that information to himself. Instead he introduced her to

Stephen. "This is Stephen Zigler, my friend and business manager. It was his idea to come in," Ty fibbed cheerfully.

Stephen reached across him to shake her hand. "The manager designation is true. The friend part is debatable."

When Grace laughed, her entire face lit with warmth. She'd already been lovely, but as her lips curled into a smile and her eyes lit… *Damn.* Ty was jealous of his friend, annoyed that Stephen, the married soon-to-be-father, had been the one to coax this from her.

"You, I like," Grace said, ignoring Ty's presence completely. "I'll see you at the reception. I really should be going…just came in to go over a few changes with the kitchen staff. Amy, their drinks are on the house."

The bartender nodded. "You're the boss."

Then Grace turned and left without another word to Ty. Stephen hooted with laughter. "There goes the winner of this cooking competition," he pronounced between chortles.

"What? Now, that's just mean," Ty complained. "You're only saying it to wound me. A great salsa verde is no basis for determining whether she can win the whole kit and caboodle."

"Oh, I wasn't basing it on that." Stephen's grin was full of admiration. "She's possibly the only woman on the planet completely immune to the Ty Beckett charm. In my book, that makes her a superhero with mystical powers. Dude, you're toast."

GRACE DROVE PAST THE MAIN building, which looked like an Italian villa, complete with a red-tiled roof and graceful fountains out front, and found a place to park. Her hands were shaking from adrenaline. And from too little sleep, she admitted to herself. She was not in top form tonight. Her father would have been disappointed in her display back at the Jalapeño. Victor Torres Senior had possessed a gift for making people feel welcome. She'd given in to her temperamental side and had been rude to Ty Beckett. What were the chances she could avoid speaking with him for the rest of the night? She wasn't even sure what she'd meant by her "spying" accusation—it wasn't as though she'd caught him sneaking into the kitchen wearing a hat and false mustache. But when she'd seen him at the bar, exuding negligent confidence as though he belonged there, as though he rightfully belonged anyplace he felt like being, she'd been intimidated. Which in turn made her angry.

She was putting that behind her now. *I am a consummate professional.* Should she happen to find herself in Ty's company, she'd be courteous and simply ignore him the rest of the time.

Right. Because ignoring a face like that would be so easy. Amy had been correct—he was even better looking in person. But what had been more startling was the sense of overwhelming familiarity Grace had felt when he'd looked at her. *He reminds me of someone.*

Grace gave herself a mental shake. Enough. Her focus needed to be on this competition, not some wandering chef with a dazzling smile and lady-killer rep. She climbed out of the car and followed the path, which twinkled with dozens of tiny white lights. There was enough illumination for her to appreciate the stone bell tower to her left and a beautifully tiled open courtyard. She imagined that later this evening, once food and drinks were served, guests would mill outside and make use of the round iron tables. It was a lovely evening, but the breeze carried a distinct chill. She was glad for the long sleeves that offset the vee neckline of her wraparound dress. Still, the filmy green fabric wasn't very thick. She should have grabbed the sweater she kept on a coatrack back in the restaurant office, but she'd been flustered when she left.

Once she opened the rounded wooden door that brought to mind stately castles, her stomach clenched in a fresh bout of nerves. Since she had the advantage of being local, knowing her way around town and not having to check in to a hotel that afternoon, she was one of the first contestants to arrive. But the two other chefs she spotted inside the huge room were both renowned in their areas of expertise—desserts and molecular gastronomy, the industry term for those who applied science to cooking in innovative ways. Talking to them was the host for *Road Trip,* Damien Craig, whom she recognized from myriad television appearances.

Behind her, the door swept open, admitting Katharine Garner and her husband, plus Ty Beckett and his business manager. Knowing that if she continued to stand in the entryway she wouldn't be able to avoid Ty, Grace made a beeline toward one of the four bars bracketing the room. There, she accepted a glass of an award-winning cabernet blend so richly delicious that she immediately began trying to compose recipes to go with it.

She closed her eyes to better savor a sip, then opened them again as she sensed someone next to her.

"Is it good?" a baritone voice asked.

She turned to smile at Damien Craig, thinking it was a shame he didn't narrate audio books. He was sort of generically handsome—*he's no Ty Beckett*—but he had an incredible voice. "Mr. Craig, nice to meet you. I'm Grace Torres. And yes, the wine is fantastic."

They stood making small talk about the vineyard, the upcoming festival and how he thought he had the best job in the world, traveling all over, meeting new people and enjoying meals prepared by legendary chefs. By the time he continued on with his social rounds, all of the contestants had arrived. Guests were grouped in clusters around the room, some standing near the large hors d'oeuvres table in the center, others chatting in corners or waiting for their wineglasses to be filled. Ty Beckett stood amid three attractive women. *Naturally.* One of them seemed to be on the show's crew, but the other two were chefs. Judging from the women's smiles and the way blonde pastry chef Phoebe Verlaine kept finding excuses to touch him, they didn't find Ty less attractive just because he was the competition.

Grace was en route to say hello to Antonio Zavalo, a chef who'd known her father, when Ty unexpectedly fell into step with her.

"We meet again," he said cheerfully.

"That tends to happen when you follow someone." As an afterthought, she added a half smile to temper the acerbic words, but he wasn't fooled.

"Are you always so prickly, Grace, or—" he lowered his voice to a conspiratorial whisper "—is this an act to keep people from knowing how much you want me?"

She nearly gaped at the outrageous comment but decided that would only encourage him. Rather than give him the satisfaction of a protest, she nodded. "Yes. Arrogant chefs who resort to mind games with their opponents are exactly my type."

The amount of sarcasm dripping from her words would have shamed a lesser man into retreat. Instead Ty's mischievous smile grew more wicked. "I knew you were crazy for me. Stephen didn't believe me."

Grace's step faltered as she studied his grin. She was experiencing that tingle of déjà vu again. Was he familiar to her because she'd seen him on television? Maybe that was it, although she still felt as if he reminded her of someone specific, someone famous whose identity was right on the tip of her brain.

"Grace!" Meeting her halfway, Antonio stepped forward to pull her into his burly arms for a warm hug. "So wonderful to see you again. How are your brothers?"

"They're…" Well, one of them was injured physically and the other was injured emotionally. "Oh, how rude of me. Antonio, do you know Ty Beckett?"

"Only by professional reputation." The older man shook Ty's hand. "Congratulations on making the semifinal round, to both of you."

"It's an honor," Ty said. "Especially when it means cooking alongside greats such as yourself. I've always looked up to you. Of course, I still plan on beating you," he added unrepentantly.

This was met with one of Antonio's deep belly laughs. "Cocky. I'd heard that about you."

"I'm afraid that, in my case, you should believe everything you hear."

Antonio clapped him on the shoulder. "Hope you aren't eliminated too soon. I have a feeling working with you around is never boring. Grace, I'll catch up with you later. For now, I want to try a glass of their port."

"I do believe he liked me," Ty said as the other man walked away. "Most people do," he added pointedly.

"Conformists," she scoffed. "I'm not into groupthink." Why was she bantering with him? What had happened to her plan of polite but remote? *Face it, remote just isn't in the Torres DNA.*

"Is that why you do fusion food?" Ty asked. "Unique combinations of flavors because you don't want to be like everyone else?"

"I'm not trying to make a social statement, just being who I am." When he looked unconvinced, she added, "I have an eclectic background. My mother is of Irish descent, my father was Hispanic. My favorite cousin was adopted as a little girl from China. My music playlists are like that, too, jumping from genre to genre. I enjoy variety."

"On that we agree, sweetheart."

Suddenly it clicked. *I know who he reminds me of!* She flashed back to her childhood, watching Indiana Jones movies with her brothers. Ty's gray-blue eyes were far too light, but his build was about the same. With his short brown hair, tousled slightly on top, and a five o'clock shadow that looked more like half past eight, he had the right mix of clean-cut masculinity and attractively scruffy. All he needed was the fedora.

Ty smirked, making her aware she'd been staring for several seconds.

Heat crept into her cheeks. "I—I was just trying to picture you with a hat and a whip."

His face went completely blank at the non sequitur. She felt a twinge of satisfaction, seeing the irrepressible Ty Beckett nonplussed.

But he recovered with a lazy half smile. "Interesting game. My turn. Want to know how I'm picturing you?"

"No!"

At that moment, Damien Craig called for everyone's attention, solidifying Grace's belief that there was a benevolent God. She sidled away from Ty, losing him in the throng as people gathered toward the front tables. Damien spoke into a portable microphone, inviting them all to sit down.

"Good evening, ladies and gentleman. I hope you're all enjoying the wonderful food and wine…and getting to know your rivals. There are ten fantastic chefs in this room tonight, each with different backgrounds and unique skill sets." He read all of their names in alphabetical order, starting with Ty and finishing with Seamus Wilson. "Unfortunately only five of you will actually compete in the events at Frederick-Fest, which begins Saturday. We'll start filming tomorrow, giving you individual and team challenges this week until we've narrowed it down to our finalists. Good luck. Remember it's an honor just to compete." He waited a beat. "Of course, it's a much bigger honor to win."

DECLINING A CUP OF after-breakfast coffee, Stephen pushed his chair back from the table and stood. His expression, a combination of sternness and awkwardness, made him look like a father leaving his teenage son at college for the first time. "Would it do any good to tell you to behave?"

Ty grinned. "You're one of the most paranoid SOBs I've ever met. What kind of trouble do you think I'm going to get into, exactly?"

"The mind boggles." Stephen was returning to Austin to be with his pregnant wife and catch up on work for his other clients, but he'd promised to bring Donna up for the festival when Ty made the finals. "You're going to be all right without a car? I could schedule a rental."

"The producers are providing group transportation, remember?" He paused, considering. "Although, with any luck, I can sweet-talk Grace Torres into showing me around town."

"I don't think so. Face it, you've finally met your match. She might be your kryptonite. Meaning you should probably stay away from her."

Ty made a noncommittal *mmm* sound but couldn't help thinking that if Stephen believed he could walk away from the challenge of befriending Grace, his manager didn't really know him at all.

Not long after Stephen left, it was time for Ty and the other chefs to meet in the hotel lobby. They were taken to the industrial kitchen of an upscale local restaurant that that was closed on Mondays. The owners, delighted by the publicity it would gain them, were letting the show use its facilities for the first challenge.

Once the chefs were gathered, Damien explained that they had a warm-up task involving local Texas wines. "You had the opportunity to learn about some local wines last night. Now let's see how you do with a blind tasting." They were given tasting notes to read, then they were shown to a table of numbered bottles with no visible labels. They sipped rieslings, cabs, chards and tempranillo, cleansing their palates between with bites of bread.

After they all turned in their sheets, Damien and one of his production assistants conferred in the corner, checking answers. The host returned to the center of the room. "As expected from chefs of your caliber, most of you did well. Katharine Garner and Grace Torres did particularly well, only transposing two of the wines. They tied for second place, beaten out by Ty Beckett."

Grace swiveled, pinning Ty with her dark gaze. "You didn't miss *any?*"

He didn't get a chance to answer before Damien responded, "Oh, he missed one of the same reds you and Katharine missed. But instead of mixing up number two and number eight, he hedged his bets by putting eight for both of them, giving him one more correct answer than either of you. As a reward, Chef Beckett, you get first pick of who you would like as your partner for today's cooking challenge."

Ty's grin widened as he pretended to debate his options. It would be undiplomatic to blurt the first name that came to mind, as if he hadn't even considered all the other fine chefs in the room. So he waited, giving the moment a significantly dramatic pause before declaring, "Grace Torres."

Chapter Three

Aware that a camera had probably panned to her the minute Ty said her name, Grace struggled to keep her face neutral. Having grown up with two brothers, there were a lot of things she'd learned to do as well as Ben and Vic—fishing, skateboarding, throwing darts. Alas, she'd never mastered a poker face. *"You might as well hand us your money the second you sit down,"* Ben had said, laughing. *"You're way too expressive."* Could everyone in the room see just how aggravated she was at the idea of working with Ty Beckett?

Ty ambled toward her, looking entirely too self-satisfied. To be fair, she doubted his smugness was directed at her. He probably woke up looking like that every day.

"There are people who would consider it an honor to be working with you," she murmured under her breath. "But you may have noticed, I don't like you." Grace had watched him work the room last night; even married Katharine Garner, who was older and far more acclaimed in her career, had favored him with girlish smiles. It was important Ty understood he couldn't twist *her* around his little finger just because of those silvery eyes and his gotta-love-me grin.

He stood beside her, watching as Damien matched up

the next two chefs. His lips barely moved as he answered, "You'll come around. I'm an acquired taste."

"Like *huitlacoche?*" she supplied helpfully, wondering if he knew about the crop by-product some considered a delicacy.

"Call me corn fungus all you like, you still have to work with me."

Don't remind me. Something about him recalled cute guys she'd known in high school, ones who'd charmed smitten girls into doing their homework. If Ty Beckett thought he was going to take creative control and relegate her to chopping and peeling…well, then he was out of his damn mind.

They were silent for a few minutes as they sized up the teams they'd be facing. In particular, the pairing of Katharine Garner and Antonio Zavalo seemed formidable. Finally it was down to noted pastry chef Jo Ying—a trim Asian woman who seemed far too skinny to cook desserts for a living—and Reed Lockhart, who'd introduced himself last night as the "token molecular gastronomist." The buzz of individual conversations filled the kitchen as chefs shook hands and expressed polite enthusiasm to be working together.

Ty grinned expectantly. "This is where you tell me that being on my team is a dream come true."

She snorted—"his" team indeed. "You aren't worried I'll try to sabotage you somehow?"

"And risk torpedoing yourself in the process?" He shook his head. "You seem like you want this pretty bad."

"I do."

His gaze turned steely, the playful spark in his eyes extinguished for the first time since she'd met him. "So do I." The uncharacteristic intensity in his expression and voice was jarring, but kind of sexy.

Not that I think he, personally, is sexy! It was more an appreciation for the trait in general: a man who knew what he wanted and had the focus to work for it. Had she underestimated him, just as Amy had warned her against?

If Ty was really as good as he told everyone he was... Adopting the adage about keeping enemies close, she decided to look at his choosing her as a strategic opportunity to see how he worked. And, hopefully, to get one step closer to her dream.

"All right!" Damien clapped his hands. "Now that everyone has a partner, it's time to explain your first challenge. Each team will be preparing a three-course meal of soup, entrée and dessert for the judges and notable guests. The dishes should represent the best of your combined areas of expertise as much as possible and must include certain ingredients inspired by Hill Country culture and crops."

A production assistant rolled a small metal cart into the room. On top of it was a trio of large ceramic boots.

"Each team will draw a slip of paper from all three boots," Damien instructed. "You must use all three items you pick, one per course. Outside of that, anything goes. Use this chance to show the judges what you're made of and why you should make it to the finals! Dinner will be served at seven-thirty tonight. The losing team," he added, "will be eliminated from the competition."

Grace's stomach clenched unpleasantly. She was the only local participant. If at any point she was "sent home," she didn't have the luxury of returning to her regular life and forgetting all about the contest. She'd be at the festival, on the sidelines, watching someone else win. *That won't happen.*

She had to do this, or her restaurant would be gone.

Ty interrupted her thoughts with an exaggerated sigh.

"Dessert! If I'd known we had to make dessert, I would have picked Phoebe or Jo." Both Jo Ying and Phoebe Verlaine were acclaimed pastry chefs, and Phoebe owned a bakery in Houston. Judging by how the blonde had poured herself over Ty at the reception, like chocolate ganache over cheesecake, she would have jumped at the chance to partner with him.

"Thanks for taking a chance on me instead," Grace said grudgingly. Growing up a short girl dwarfed by her classmates, she'd spent more than one elementary-school PE period waiting uncomfortably to be selected for a basketball or kickball team. While she hadn't appreciated Ty's comment last night that he'd never heard of her, she was one of the lesser-known competitors. "Why *did* you choose me?"

"Because you and I are going to be very good together." He tapped his temple. "The Beckett Instinct, it's never wrong."

Caught between the urge to grin and roll her eyes, she instead returned her attention to the chefs drawing their ingredient assignments. Phoebe and Stuart Capriotti got pecans, barbecue sauce and sauerkraut, none of which did much to heighten Phoebe's dessert advantage. Chef Camellia Stone, a vegetarian, groaned aloud at her slip that read Angus Beef.

"We'll trade you for that!" Ty volunteered.

"The hell you will," Camellia's partner, Seamus, said good-naturedly.

"Are you picking for us?" Grace asked Ty.

His immediate "not a chance" surprised her—he seemed like someone who preferred to take charge. But then he added, "If we get crappy ingredients, I want to blame you."

"There are no crappy ingredients in the Hill Country,"

she informed him tartly. But she knew he would have liked the chance at steak—the first article she remembered ever seeing about him had called him the Whiz Kid of the Grill. Based on the number of chocolatiers and fudge shops in Fredericksburg alone, she suspected chocolate would be one of the assigned ingredients. What else was waiting in those boots?

"Beckett and Torres," Damien said. "Who's doing the honors?"

"Me." Chin raised, Grace stepped forward and stuck her hand in the first boot. She unfolded the piece of paper and read, "Poblano." Half a dozen uses for the pepper immediately sprang to mind and she reached into the second boot. "Goat cheese." She'd purchased goat cheese from a local dairy for the restaurant plenty of times. "And pears."

They were great ingredients that left their team lots of latitude on what to prepare. Grace's enthusiasm soared. When she returned to Ty, she could tell by his smile that he felt the same way.

"We've got this in the bag," he whispered. "I already know the perfect entrée."

Her eyebrows shot up. "What a coincidence. So do I."

NORMALLY SPENDING TIME IN his hotel room with a beautiful woman—one who knew about food, no less—would sound like Ty's idea of heaven. But the past half hour with Grace Torres had sent his blood pressure blasting off like a space shuttle. Were other teams having this problem? After they'd been given their challenges, they'd been turned loose to plan independently. How many of his opponents were already at the designated market, working through their budget for tonight's menu?

"You're being needlessly stubborn," he informed Grace from his seat at the desk. When it had first become clear that she was resisting his ideas, he'd employed the patented Beckett charm. But so far, Stephen's observation had held true: she was immune. Ty had abandoned the smile in favor of arguing outright. He might have found the experience strangely liberating if the outcome didn't affect his career.

Grace didn't even pause in her pacing. "How am I being any more stubborn than you?" she demanded. "Steak with poached pears! It's lame."

"It's delicious," he corrected. "If we had time, I'd borrow the kitchen at your restaurant and make you eat your words, but we don't."

She muttered a few phrases in Spanish, then sighed. "Maybe I shouldn't have said 'lame.' But even you have to admit, poached pears are predictable. And at least one other team is already doing steak."

"Their attempt will probably make ours even better in comparison. Camellia's a vegetarian!"

Again with the stream of Spanish.

"Cut that out," he insisted. "I feel like I need damn subtitles for this discussion."

"You're conveniently forgetting Seamus was a chef for three years at a steak house," she said. "Look, I get that you're Lord of the Lighter Fluid or whatever, but steak can't be the only thing in your comfort zone."

"I have just as many things in my repertoire as you do, lady. Just because I don't throw together weird flavors for shock value like some fusionists doesn't mean I'm a one-trick pony."

She halted, her hands going to her nicely rounded hips. "Only someone with an extremely limited palate would find pear salsa shocking."

Ty grunted dismissively; it wasn't the salsa that bothered him as much as what she wanted to put it on. "You expect to win with chicken tacos?" He rocked his chair back on two legs. "Now who isn't thinking outside the box?"

"These dishes are supposed to represent who we are as chefs," she reminded him. "Both of us. You can grill the chicken, and the pear salsa is representative of the way I like to blend flavors. Don't you dare try to muscle me out of what we serve."

He plowed a hand through his hair, aware it was probably standing on end. Thank goodness she'd wanted to talk privately to deter friendly locals from interrupting, because he'd completely abandoned the public image he worked so hard to project. If the suits making the decision on whether to green-light his show saw him like this, short-tempered and disheveled, he'd be screwed. *Get it together, Beckett.* He and Grace both had the same goal, to kick the other teams' butts, so how hard could it be to find common ground?

"We seem to have lost sight of the fact that we're on the same side." He offered her a wry grin. "I'm guessing you're the oldest child in your family. Used to bossing everyone else around?"

Her espresso eyes narrowed. "Youngest, actually. You the oldest?"

"Only child."

"Well, *that* explains a lot."

"All right, so we're both control freaks." He lowered his chair back to the hardwood floor. "Here's what I suggest as a compromise—you take the soup and the dessert, and I do the entrée. We help each other with any necessary prep but, creatively, we stay out of each other's way."

She tapped her index finger against her lips. After a moment, Ty realized he was staring and wished she'd stop drawing attention to her mouth. He was suddenly far too intent on the curve of her full bottom lip.

He cleared his throat. "What do you think?"

"I'm torn," she admitted. "You took the main course for yourself."

"Giving you double the opportunity to wow the judges with your epicurean genius," he said diplomatically.

"And double the work?"

"I'll even let you pick which two ingredients you want first," he offered.

"Meaning that our entrée will be either steak with pears, steak with goat cheese or steak with poblano peppers."

He ground his teeth. "Anyone ever tell you you're a real pain in the ass?"

Surprisingly she grinned, her expression the most affectionate he'd ever received from her. "My brothers, on a daily basis."

"They have my sympathy," he quipped.

"Okay, you get the entrée," she said. "But I'm taking the pears and goat cheese. Can you do a poblano justice?"

"Have a little faith, sweetheart."

She nodded to the hotel stationery near his elbow. "Can you tear me off a sheet of that? I want to jot down a quick grocery list before we go."

"Would it save time if I drive and you make your list in the car?"

"You're not driving my car. Besides, I'm the one who knows how to get around town."

Both valid points. "Guess I'm just used to being in the driver's seat," he said with an easy shrug.

"Then this will be a character-building experience for you."

He handed her the piece of paper for her notes and

turned at the desk to jot his own list. But his thoughts lingered on Grace rather than the challenge. Interesting woman—his smiles and flattery had no effect on her whatsoever, but when he'd called her a pain in the ass, she'd capitulated. *Focus.* He gave himself a mental shake and concentrated on his list.

But once they were in her dented two-door hatchback, on the way to the store, he gave in to his curiosity, wanting to know more about her life and what made her tick. "You mentioned brothers earlier. Two, right?"

She cut her gaze toward him. "How did you know that?"

"There was a picture at the restaurant," he said. "Of a little girl standing between two taller boys. I didn't realize it was you at first, but when you said brothers... So you grew up in the restaurant business?"

"Yeah, the Jalapeño was my second home. By the time I hit elementary school, Ben and Vic were already busy with middle-school extracurriculars. While Mom was running them to and from practices and games, I'd go to the restaurant to do my homework and stuff myself on *sopaipillas.* One of the waiters used to help me with math, and Mac, our bartender before he retired, used to drill me on spelling words. But the best part was being in the kitchen, getting to taste-test for my father."

Ty squelched a pang of envy, trying not to recall his own lonely, hungry childhood. *It doesn't matter now. That's not who you are.*

Shoving aside his past, he kept the conversation on her family. "Your dad must be proud of you, following in his footsteps and becoming a chef."

Grief contorted her features, and he could see her struggle to regain composure. Her face was almost painfully expressive. Just looking at her could feel like an invasion of privacy. He turned toward the window, watching tourists walk across intersections. He'd deduced that her father was dead long before she spoke.

"Dad passed away three years ago. I thought I'd finished mourning him, but then when Mom…"

"You lost her, too?" Ty was horrified by the Pandora's box he'd unwittingly opened.

She swallowed hard. "No, not the way you mean. She has early-onset Alzheimer's."

"Sorry." He wasn't sure if the trite word was meant to be a condolence for what she was going through or an apology for bringing up her family in the first place.

His usual talent for effortless small talk deserted him. Claustrophobia gripped him. He wished he could be anywhere but inside this car. Or, if he had to be here, he wished Stephen was, too. Ty excelled at flirting, getting his way and perfectly searing meat. He could look into a camera and make an unseen audience feel as if he were connecting with them, but it was a superficial illusion. When it came to actually relating to anyone, his business manager was far more skilled.

With a sniff, Grace swiped the side of her hand beneath her eye. "This is the longest I've ever heard you go without talking."

"I do like the sound of my own voice," he agreed. He was more than happy to discuss his character flaws if it kept them out of the quicksand of her personal tragedies.

"Well, if you've been stewing because you're afraid the weepy chef is too emotional to carry her weight on this challenge, I promise you, I'm up to the task."

He blinked, startled by her perception of him. He might not be deep, but he wasn't heartless, either. "That honestly hadn't crossed my mind, Grace."

"Really?" She assessed him with a sidelong glance.

"Sometimes, with my brothers…they treat me as if having feelings is a liability somehow, makes me fragile. I'm going to prove them wrong when I win this competition."

Hopefully second place would be enough to make her point to her siblings. Because Ty had every intention of beating her. He said nothing, glad that for now at least, for this one challenge, they could work toward a joint victory. But after that, it would be a return to the philosophy he'd clung to since adolescence.

Every man for himself.

Chapter Four

Grace's index finger hovered over the pulse control of the food processor. "Sorry," she said with saccharine-sweet contrition, "can't hear you." Then she jabbed the button again and the blade *whirred* to life.

From the other side of the counter, Ty smirked. They both knew that the second the appliance stopped, he'd go back to his heckling. He'd been teasing her all afternoon and, although she'd do the unthinkable and buy salsa in a jar before she ever admitted it, she appreciated his irreverent playfulness. It kept her nerves from getting the best of her and helped her move past the melancholy she'd felt this morning when discussing her family.

As soon as the motor slowed and the noise died, Ty glanced up from the large pot of chowder he was stirring, which smelled like peppery-scented heaven. "Now would be a good time for you to admit you were completely wrong, by the way."

Keeping her expression deadpan was a struggle in the face of his contagious grin. Apparently her partner's charisma was like radioactivity—the longer you were exposed, the more pronounced the effects. "Fine, you didn't make steak," she acknowledged. "You want an award for that?"

His blue-gray eyes glinted. "What are you offering?"

She considered throwing a blackberry at him.

He pointed toward the chowder, his smile fading into temporary earnestness. "You want to try this one last time before we start plating?"

They'd drawn numbers earlier in the evening to determine the order in which they'd serve the judges. Phoebe Verlaine and Stuart Capriotti had just presented their food, Reed Lockhart and Jo Ying were plating now, then it would be Grace and Ty's turn.

She shook her head. "We're good to go." They'd both tried each other's dishes, and she was confident they'd nailed the recipes. Continuing to mess with the food was a rookie mistake that could lead to overseasoning and muddled flavors.

She was really excited about their three-course meal and a bit surprised by how well they'd worked together. Since her father's death, she'd grown accustomed to running the kitchen of the Jalapeño, and it was refreshing to brainstorm with someone truly knowledgeable about food. Ben and Amy normally limited their input to "*mmm*" and Victor couldn't help automatically calculating ingredient costs. Grace and Ty had been tasting each other's dishes, offering small suggestions when warranted, but there hadn't been much tampering. She'd half expected Ty would need to put his stamp on everything that came out of the kitchen, but when he'd tried the filling for her dessert, he'd simply said, "Can't improve on perfection."

We could win this. She was still worried about Katharine and Antonio, who had more combined experience than any other pair, but she thought her and Ty's chances were excellent. Their first course would be her spicy butternut-and-pear soup, followed by his grilled shellfish on a bed of creamy poblano-and-corn chowder. Then the finishing touch—Grace's goat-cheese-and-blackberry empanadas with a nutty glaze. It offered sweetness without the overwhelming richness of that triple-chocolate tart Phoebe had prepared.

Grace began ladling soup into the judge's bowls, finishing each with a decorative swirl of seasoned crème fraîche and a wafer-thin slice of pear.

"Nervous?" Ty looked pointedly at her hands, which were shaking. "I think we're going to kick ass, personally."

"So do I." She made a fist and squeezed, willing her fingers to cooperate. "It's more excitement than nerves. When it's something I care about this much, I just get… keyed-up sometimes."

Could he understand that? Smooth-talking Ty Beckett didn't seem the type to get jittery about anything.

"Tell you what," he drawled. "After we wrap this tonight, I'll buy you a drink to celebrate. Take me somewhere that has a pool table or air-hockey or whatever so you can burn off this extra energy. Maybe a dance floor."

She experienced a too-vivid picture of Ty pulling her into his arms. *Not a chance in hell.* There was an uncrossable line between "keeping your enemy close" and flat-out courting disaster. No matter how their challenge ended tonight, tomorrow morning they'd be opponents again.

"Darts," she blurted. "I like darts."

He affected a look of mock-panic. "Wait, only this morning you were telling me you don't like me. Now you want me to arm you with sharp missiles? Should I be worried?"

"Just make sure we win so I'm in a really good mood before I start throwing."

SEAMUS WILSON, IN CONTRAST to his partner Camellia's sulky silence, tried to accept defeat with a joke. "Guess

I should have traded you for that Angus, after all," he told Ty.

Ty shook the man's hand. "We all have off-days, buddy." It was a tactful fib. Personally Ty hadn't allowed himself the luxury of a bad day in over a decade. The success he'd dreamed of for so long was nearly in his grasp, and he wasn't about to let anything jeopardize it.

Still, he waited until the other teams had left the challenge kitchen before he allowed himself to gloat fully.

He took Grace by the shoulders and whirled her in a small, triumphant circle. "Hot damn, we did it!"

Her dark eyes shone with pleasure. "I can't stop smiling." In a voice husky with pride, she marveled over their accomplishment. "We just beat Antonio Zavalo and Katharine Garner! I may never stop smiling."

Antonio and Katharine had been their stiffest competition. One of the judges had said they might have won if they hadn't used two of the signature items from the famed menu of Katharine's New York restaurant.

"The food was every bit as excellent as we would have expected from you, but you didn't stretch yourselves. You merely took already proven recipes and tossed in a few additional items, making the Hill Country ingredients seem more like afterthought than inspiration."

Camellia and Seamus, on the other hand, might have been overly ambitious, especially with their dessert. When complications had arisen with their peach soufflé, they'd become distracted trying to save it. As a result, the steaks had overcooked—a crime against Angus, in Ty's opinion.

Grace took a step back, unbuttoning her chef's jacket. "We've got to celebrate! And eat. I'm starving. Are you starving?"

He had been, before she'd shrugged out of her jacket. Now he was distracted by the sight of her in the red tank top. The scooped neckline dipped down beneath her collarbone, providing a tantalizing glimpse of cleavage. She pulled a cropped black sweater out of her duffel bag.

"Ty? We still on for grabbing a bite and toasting victory?" She reached both hands to the top of her head, working at an elastic band until her hair tumbled free over her shoulders.

"Oh, yeah." But the words were automatic. He'd barely heard the question, not that it mattered. The way she looked right now—eyes sparkling, her smiling face framed by the thick, inky waves of her hair—she could probably get a man to agree to just about anything.

GRACE SWIPED A SWEET POTATO fry through the spicy honey mustard on her plate, appreciating the way the flavors counterbalanced each other. "I feel funny about bringing you here," she told Ty, her voice raised in deference to the overhead music blaring in the small bar.

"Funny?" he repeated. "Why?"

She probably wouldn't have been able to hear him except that their table was only about a foot and a half in diameter, forcing them to sit in close proximity. She'd accidentally grazed his leg with her own, and they were near enough that his body heat was keeping them both warm. It was funny—she'd spent all afternoon and much of the evening in a kitchen with multiple stoves and ovens running but couldn't remember feeling as flushed as she did now, seated beneath a lazily spinning ceiling fan.

Frowning, she tried to remember what she'd been about to say.

She averted her gaze. Somehow it was easier to think when she wasn't looking directly at him. "It's not exactly a five-star restaurant," she admitted. "The cooks do okay with the menu they have, and people come here more for the pool tables and range of beers on tap than for the food. But you just spent the day in the company of some of the best chefs in Texas!"

"Sweetheart, I *am* one of the best chefs in Texas. You think that stops me from going out and enjoying a quick burger now and then?" He gestured toward his half-empty plate. "You haven't heard me complain."

The mild sense of relief she felt surprised her. Had she actually been worried about his opinion? It was true she'd grown up in the area and loved her hometown, but why should she care what Ty Beckett thought of his time here? As soon as *Road Trip* was finished filming their competition segments, he would move on to whatever awaited him next.

"I've read articles about you," she began.

"My fame precedes me."

She ignored the interjection. "Seems like you're something of a drifter in the culinary world. Surely a chef of your caliber has had opportunities to open your own place?"

As soon as the press release had gone out that she'd been selected for the cooking show, locals had been congratulating her and offering moral support. And, while she didn't like to dwell on the dark days right after her dad's death, she'd been touched by the outpouring of sympathy from town citizens. Did Ty get lonely, not having that sense of community? Then again, having witnessed him flirt with women both on television and in person, she supposed he found ways to alleviate loneliness.

"My own place?" He shook his head, looking vaguely alarmed by the idea. "Restaurants are never a sure thing, even for chefs of my caliber." He echoed her words with a grin, raising his hand slightly to salute her with his glass.

It was true that many new restaurants failed, even good

ones. But she couldn't imagine he was afraid of the odds. Ty Beckett seemed too sure of himself to fear anything.

"Besides," he continued, "I don't have to tell you how much responsibility a restaurant is! How many days do you get to just have fun in the kitchen, play with new ideas without worrying about mortgage payments or staff issues or advertising?"

His question hit too close to home, and even she could hear the cranky undertone in her voice when she asked, "So you're just in it to have fun?"

"You say that like it's a bad thing." He shrugged unabashedly. "I'm enjoying the hell out of my life, and I'm not hurting anyone."

She had no response that wouldn't sound wildly sarcastic, so instead, she pushed her plate toward the center of the table. "I'm all done, whenever you're ready for that game of darts." Suddenly Grace found herself in the mood to throw something.

TY COULDN'T REMEMBER WHEN he'd had dinner with a less predictable woman—or one with better aim. To say he'd lost their first game of 'Round the Clock was a bit of an understatement. *I got my ass handed to me.* Though she'd resisted any urge to mock him outright, her eyes had danced with humor as she suggested handicapping herself for the second game. As much as Ty detested losing, it was good to see her spirits rise again.

When they'd left the challenge kitchen tonight, she'd been vibrating with giddy energy from their win, downright bubbly in the car. Yet she'd tensed up again as they ate, leaving him feeling almost as if he'd done something wrong, which was ridiculous. As they'd left their table, there had been a painfully rigid set to her spine. Now, however, she moved with fluid grace that was a joy to watch.

He marveled at her most recent throw. "I'm not sure I've ever seen anyone with such merciless precision." He supposed many people could train themselves to hit the bull's-eye consistently, but after winning the initial throw that determined who went first and who got to pick the game, Grace had chosen a variation that required mastery of every section of the board. "I might be a little scared of you now."

She grinned over her shoulder. "Flatterer." After she nailed the bull's-eye with her second dart, she commented, "My oldest brother, Victor, can add forty numbers in his head with the same accuracy as a calculator. He said once that he was gifted with precision, that Ben—who tracks down criminals for a living—was blessed with intuition, and that I..." She hit the double bull's-eye, putting him out of his misery. "Got the best of both."

The poetry of her timing, skill and wicked grin hit his system like a fiery shot of tequila. With some disoriented surprise, Ty realized he was turned on. For someone with his competitive drive, it was an unheard of response to losing. Well, except maybe for that one game of strip poker shortly after his twenty-first birthday, but that was different.

He had a sudden visual of Grace peering at him over a hand of cards, wearing the same smile she had now. And very little else. His brain almost short-circuited at the thought.

"You are one dangerous lady," he said softly.

Luckily she had no idea he meant it. *"Muy peligrosa,"* she agreed cheerfully as she retrieved her darts. "I keep trying to tell my roommate that!"

"Roommate?" For no logical reason, his mind went straight to some of the romantic comedies he'd seen with dates. Movies where an attractive heroine lived with an attractive guy, but for reasons Ty could never fathom, neither of them acted on their obvious attraction until practically the end of the film. The idea of Grace—

"Amy," she said. "You've met her. She's the bartender at the Jalapeño."

His shoulders eased. "The one with the butterfly tattoo?"

Grace nodded, exchanging the darts in her hand for the drink she'd left on the wooden rail. "She moved here from Austin and, selfishly speaking, she couldn't have come at a better time. She was bunking at a bed-and-breakfast while she looked for a more permanent living situation. Meanwhile, I had to move because…" She faltered. "I'd been living at home, helping take care of Mom after Dad died. But then we—my brothers and I—decided that she needed more help. Better help."

Her voice trembled, and her eyes were suspiciously bright.

"Hey. It's okay." He reached for her, meaning to squeeze her arm or pat her on the back, something innocuously encouraging. But his body took it a step further, pulling her against him in a hug. *Beckett, you ass.* Was he really taking advantage of her mother's illness to hold her? He couldn't have let go any faster if she'd been a burning hot pan he'd mistakenly touched.

"Sorry," he said curtly.

Her forehead crinkled as she frowned at him. "Don't be. That was…sweet."

The hell it was, he thought guiltily. "I don't do 'sweet,'" he told her, shuddering for effect. He paused a beat before asking lightly, "How do you know it wasn't just an excuse to touch a beautiful woman?"

She chuckled.

"No, really. I've already been working an elaborate

strategy to make it look like I suck at darts so you'd put your arms around me and correct my form. You don't think I'm really as bad as our two games would suggest?"

She smirked. "Well, you were pretty convincing. Want to play one more before we call it a night?"

After the practice of the first two rounds, he did far better in the final match, almost—but not quite—giving her a run for her money.

"Maybe you *don't* actually suck," Grace allowed.

The narrowed gap between them wasn't just because he'd improved, though. She was no longer throwing with the same effortless accuracy. Her expression was distracted, and her heart wasn't in the game. Though it was his turn, he didn't step toward the throw line.

Instead he asked, "Still thinking about your mom?" He immediately wished he could take back the words. Despite their camaraderie today, they weren't truly friends—he'd probably never see her again after next week. So why was he prying into personal matters? Evenings with weepy females didn't rate high on his list of good times.

She sniffed. "There you go, being sweet again."

"You have to stop saying that," he grumbled.

"I'm visiting her in the morning," Grace said, belatedly answering his question. "There's always this awful moment when I knock on her door and wonder…I wonder if—" She reached for her water, but he gently took the glass from her hand.

"Here." He picked up his beer and curled her fingers around the bottle. "You look like you need something a little stronger."

Her gaze grateful, she took a generous drink. When she gave him back the beer, her composure seemed restored, if not her concentration. "I concede," she said with a wave in the direction of the dartboard. "You win."

He scowled at her. "Huh."

"What's wrong?"

"Usually I love to win. I live for success. But it turns out, winning just because your opponent gives up isn't any fun."

She considered this. "All right. Maybe we'll call this a rain check instead of a forfeit, then. You want another crack at victory some other time?"

"Deal."

Once they were back in her car, she apologized for putting a damper on his evening. "Sorry I wasn't more fun tonight."

"You have a lot on your mind," he said tactfully. "And Grace? I hope your visit tomorrow goes well."

"Thank you. I—" She cleared her throat, then changed the subject. "Enough about me! What about your parents? Either of them cook, professionally or for fun?"

Ty gritted his teeth. She'd found the one topic of conversation that made him even less comfortable than her family—his. "I was raised by a single mom, so I have no idea if my father cooked." He had no idea who his father *was*. "But I suppose my mother was one of my inspirations." It was true, even if the ways in which the truck stop waitress had inspired him were a lot different than what Grace might assume.

"I guess if it was just the two of you, you're pretty close?" Grace asked.

For once, Ty was at a total loss for a reply. He didn't want to say "no" and sound hostile. He harbored no ill will toward Beth Beckett—hell, he mailed her quarterly checks.

Well, he had Stephen do it, but that amounted to the same thing. The expedient option was simply to fib and say "yep," but the lie wouldn't come. Probably because if he told Grace they'd been close, she'd expect some sort of endearing anecdote about how it had been him and Beth against the world.

"Look, I hope the visit with your mom goes well," he reiterated. "But I wasn't trying to turn this into a big sharing session, so drop it."

Grace whipped her head toward him. Even in the dark, her startled expression was easy to read.

Ty was a bit startled himself. He'd had media training, which involved tactics for deflecting questions an interviewee didn't want to answer. So why had he resorted to sarcastic bluntness? "Sorry," he muttered. "Long day."

"I understand." On the surface, her words might have been conciliatory, but there was an acid bite to her tone. "After all, I was there for the whole thing."

Silence descended like an oppressive fog. Ty had never been so eager for a car ride to end. As they pulled into the small parking lot of the hotel, it was all he could do not to hurl himself from the moving vehicle. Instead he unbuckled his seat belt with unhurried movements and gave Grace a polite smile.

He even managed a neutral, "See you tomorrow," before throwing open his door.

By tomorrow, he vowed, he would have his head back in the game. No more worrying about the state of the Torres family. No more dwelling on Grace's soft, lush body or the glint in her eyes when she let herself return his teasing. He tapped his temple with the heel of his palm, as if dislodging the mental image.

Watching her play darts during that third game tonight, he'd been given a reminder of how distraction could knock a competitor out of the running. This was his professional future on the line here, not an insignificant bar game. He'd come too damn far in his life to risk losing his edge now.

GRACE PARKED OUTSIDE THE assisted-living complex. If she were lucky, she'd have enough time for an unhurried breakfast with her mom before she had to cross town for today's cooking challenge. Maybe this visit was exactly what she needed—the tangible reminder of how important her family was, all the reasons that securing the restaurant's financial future was so important—to get her refocused on winning. In retrospect, Grace couldn't imagine why she'd agreed to go out with Ty Beckett last night. She should have thanked him for his part in securing their victory, then gone home to rest up for another big day in the kitchen.

Their dinner was definitely a mistake. She didn't know what had unbalanced her more, his instances of almost tender consideration or how he bit off her head at the end of the night. As she locked her car, she told herself that neither his kindness nor his prickly flare of temper mattered. Not in the long run. She crossed the lot, letting the March breeze blow away any lingering mixed emotions about Chef Beckett.

Walking into the lobby of the Gunther Gardens complex always caused a stab of resentment. It was fine for *Tía* Maria to voluntarily rent an apartment on the premises, but Grace hated that her mother was here out of necessity, not choice. Grace went through her usual ritual of looking around, assuring herself yet again that this was a nice place.

Since Maria already lived on the grounds, Gunther Gardens had seemed like a logical new home for Colleen. But, just to be sure, Grace and her brothers had investigated other options, too. One place, set apart by its institutional decor and eye-watering disinfectant fumes, had been too much like a hospital. Another, with its shabbily furnished front parlor and a game room featuring a

scratched Ping-Pong table on the verge of collapse, re-
sembled a third-rate college dorm. The main lobby of
Gunther Gardens, however, was walled in pale stone. The
high ceiling and many windows provided plenty of space
and light. Well-padded navy-and-gold chairs, which tied
together the gold-flecked tile and the chocolate-and-navy
window treatments, were high quality without being uncomfortably formal. And Grace had personally sampled
breakfasts, lunches, dinners *and* holiday desserts in the
complex's dining room before she declared Gunther Gardens good enough for her mother.

Mustering a smile for Ida at the front desk, Grace
signed the requisite visitation forms.

"Morning," Ida chirped. "I haven't seen your mama
today, but after dinner last night she played checkers with
Floyd Emmett. She's starting to make friends."

"That's good to hear." Grace had been worried about
Colleen's anxiety around people, so far removed from the
vivacious woman who'd once been the life of every party.

Although some Alzheimer's patients became increasingly belligerent, Colleen Torres was paradoxically more
subdued. Then again, as Colleen's doctor was prone to
reminding them, "If you've met one person with Alzheimer's, you've met *one* person with Alzheimer's." Each
individual's case was different.

As Grace started down the hall that led to living quar-
ters, Ida called after her, "Good luck on that cooking
show! Paul and I can't wait to watch it on TV."

The reminder of today's waiting challenge made her
stomach knot. As thrilled as she was to have won yesterday, that meant there wasn't much room for improvement.
Could she win twice in a row, and, if not, would she feel
like she'd lost ground with the judges? *Speaking of food...*
Grace mentally kicked herself. Why hadn't she gotten up

in the middle of the night to cook some goodies for her mom? Since she'd been tossing and turning anyway, she might as well have made better use of her time. But she'd stubbornly kept trying to fall asleep, knowing she would need to be in top form for whatever task the producers threw at them today.

Please don't let it be a team challenge. Her evening with Ty had left her emotionally raw and the kitchen had always been her refuge. Today, she just wanted to be left alone so she could slip into her Zen-like creative zone without interference.

Grace stopped at her mom's door. With a tight swallow, she raised her fist to knock. This was the moment she dreaded each visit. She lived in panicked anticipation of the day Colleen Torres opened the door and didn't recognize her.

So far, it had only happened with Maria. As Grace's aunt tried to remind Colleen who she was, it had become clear Colleen remembered having a sister-in-law but was envisioning her at a much younger age. She hadn't been able to reconcile the seventy-four-year-old woman to the image in her mind.

Maybe that would never happen with Grace—and she knew, rationally, that even if it did, it wasn't a commentary on how much her mother loved her. She just prayed that if the day came when her mom didn't know her, she'd handle it in a way that wouldn't alarm or upset Colleen. The worst times weren't when something slipped Colleen's mind altogether, but rather when she was painfully aware that an important memory eluded her.

This morning, however, Colleen met her with a warm smile. "Gracie!"

"Morning, Mom." Grace kissed her mother's cheek,

breathing in the familiar vanilla scent of her favorite lotion.

Now that Colleen lived in Gunther Gardens, her laundry was done for her; it had taken Grace a few visits to realize what seemed "off." Her mother's clothes, which she'd washed with the same detergent for decades and line-dried in their backyard, no longer smelled the same. But Grace dutifully purchased the soap, shampoo and lotion her mom liked.

"You're all dressed for breakfast," Grace noted. That was a good sign, even if the outfit was a bit eccentric. There were days when Colleen had to be coaxed to get out of bed, much less her small apartment. "The colors are very cheerful." Her mom had paired a Christmas sweater with yellow linen walking shorts and sparkly rhinestone sandals.

"*You* don't look cheerful." Colleen frowned at her, the expression of maternal concern the same one Grace had seen throughout her adolescence whenever she'd struggled with a class, a recipe or a crush. "Is everything okay, love?"

"Absolutely fine," Grace said, hoping she sounded more convincing than she felt. "I just didn't sleep very well last night."

Her mother clucked her tongue reproachfully. "But you need your rest! You have that cooking contest coming up soon."

Grace smiled, touched that her mom remembered the competition. "A cup of coffee and a good breakfast will set me right again. Ready?"

Though Colleen loved tasting new culinary creations, she'd always had a much smaller appetite than her hearty husband and growing children. In the dining room, she consented to an order of French toast dusted with pow-

dered sugar, as long as Grace promised to help her eat it.
While they shared their food, Colleen talked about some
of the tenants she'd met. It seemed Ida had been right;
Grace's mother was making friends.

Leaning forward, Colleen brushed Grace's hair away
from her face. It brought to mind countless Sunday morn-
ings, when the whole family was seated in a pew waiting
for Mass to start and Colleen would affectionately fuss
with her daughter's hair, patting it into place or straightening a bow. "Feel better now that you have some food in
you?" Colleen asked.

"Much." Overall, Grace's outlook on life had improved
drastically since she'd first arrived.

"Good." Colleen lowered her voice to a whisper. "Just
between you and me, do you know who else looks like
she hasn't been sleeping well? Natalie."

"Victor's wife?" Grace asked blankly. "You've seen
her?"

"She came by on Saturday. Or maybe Friday. No, it was
Saturday. But she had dark circles under her eyes. Looked
like she might have been crying."

Grace bit her lip, wondering if her mother recalled that
Natalie and Victor had separated. Even once the divorce
was finalized, Grace herself would have trouble not thinking of Natalie as family. The two women had been sisters
for almost a decade. Should she call Natalie? They'd been
close, but now their friendship seemed almost disloyal to
Vic.

"She told me not to worry about her," Colleen continued. "That she'd been feeling a little puny, but it was nothing serious. You know what this means, don't you?"

"Uhh…"

"I bet they're going to have another baby! In all the
time they've been married, the only times I've known

Natalie to be under the weather were her pregnancies. And the crying? Every expectant woman succumbs to hormones from time to time. You'll see, when it's your turn."

"My turn?" Grace parroted. She had too much on her plate to even hold a boyfriend right now; the possibility of marriage and children were so far on the horizon that—

That Mom might not get to enjoy them. When and if Grace did marry, would her mother be able to help her plan the big day, bask in all the festivities the way she had during Victor and Natalie's engagement? Would Colleen ever get to hold a grandchild her daughter had borne?

Grace's forced swallow of hot coffee did nothing to melt away the lump in her throat. *Whatever else happens, I'll have boxes full of pictures to show my children and a lifetime worth of memories and funny stories.* She could consider herself lucky. She'd grown up in a boisterous, outgoing family full of people who adored one another. Not everyone had that.

Despite her resolve to put Ty Beckett out of her mind, she couldn't help recalling their car ride last night, when she'd asked if he and his mother were close. His silence had spoken volumes. And the way he'd snapped at her afterward? In almost every circumstance, from his televised interviews to his trying to win her over, he poured on charm thicker than maple syrup. For someone like him to be so abrupt, she must have really struck a nerve.

She couldn't imagine what her own life would have been without the bond she'd shared with her parents. Her father had shaped the chef she'd become, and her mother's unconditional love had been a constant her entire life. Had Ty been denied the elemental relationships every child should know? It was impossible not to pity the boy he'd been.

But that didn't mean she planned to go easy on the man he was now. She had to defeat Ty—and Antonio and Katharine and the rest—or lose yet another piece of her world.

Chapter Five

Even though Ty had his back to the rest of the room, chatting with a couple of the contestants in a corner, he knew the instant Grace entered the kitchen. It was as if the barometric pressure suddenly changed, as if the air were electrically charged with a coming storm. He temporarily lost his place in the conversation but managed not to turn around. It took Herculean effort. His instincts clamored for him to smile at her, to talk to her. *Let it go, Beckett.*

Just as some people were obsessive about getting the last word in an argument, Ty was a bit fanatical about making sure the final impression he left with someone was good. In restaurants, if a dessert was awful or a waiter was rude at the end of the meal, patrons went home with a negative takeaway and might never return. Because of networking, the culinary world was a small one. Even if his and Grace's professional paths didn't directly cross again, they were likely to have mutual acquaintances in the industry. After he won this competition, he didn't want to leave Fredericksburg knowing there was a colleague here who hated him.

Although he didn't intend to do anything as drastic as *apologize,* there were subtler ways to smooth over last night's awkward parting. If he asked how her visit had gone this morning, demonstrating that he'd listened and cared, would she forgive his brief detour through Jackass Junction at the end of their evening?

"Good morning, chefs!" Damien's baritone cut through Ty's mental debate. "I'm sure you've all been wondering what our next big challenge is. Today, you'll be pairing the perfect bite with the perfect beverage."

He directed their attention to the diverse assortment of bottles lining the counters—from Tito's vodka and the winning brand of the most recent Texas Tequila Throwdown to Shiner longnecks and Messina Hof wines. All the spirits were products of the Lone Star State. Each chef would choose a regional libation, whether they served it straight from the bottle or in a mixed drink, and devise an *amuse-bouche,* chefspeak for tiny hors d'oeuvre. Damien outlined their budget and the two markets in the area where they'd be allowed to shop. They'd be transported in the trio of official *Road Trip* passenger vans, and Ty found himself scheming for a seat near Grace as the chefs were ushered toward the parking lot.

Again, that inner voice advised him to simply stay away from her. It was the less complicated option. But Ty had never been particularly good at taking advice, even from himself. He felt compelled to talk to her.

Donna Zigler, Stephen's wife, had once teased him about his "pathological need to be liked." Stephen had scoffed, "If he's so worried about getting people to like him, how do you explain his Texas-size obnoxious streak?" If Ty had been the type of person who ever discussed his past, he could have told him that the two traits weren't mutually exclusive.

In the section of south Texas where he'd grown up, he hadn't been the only impoverished child. But some days it had felt like that. The Benito family and the Jessups were poor, too, but they'd had three and five kids respectively. At school, the siblings looked out for each other and students learned fast not to heckle a Jessup on the playground about hand-me-down clothes or a Benito for not being able to contribute a dollar for a class pizza party. But no one had Ty's back. He'd learned that if he heckled himself first, he could head off some of the bullying. Plus, the more he made others laugh, the more they liked him.

He never had a single best friend; he'd invested in dozens of casual friendships that led to kids sharing an uneaten half of a sandwich or asking him over for dinner. A select few even owned pools and invited him to swim during the summer, which beat the hell out of roasting alive in his trailer. It was as a guest in those homes that he'd begun turning on the charm. His schoolyard shenanigans and class-clown behavior, he quickly realized, were not the best way to win over parents. Teresa Beck was one of many moms who had grown to adore him. For an entire school year, he'd walked to her house many Wednesday afternoons, always managing to be about five minutes ahead of when her son was dropped off after his Scout meeting.

"Oh, George isn't home yet, but come on in and have some cookies or a bowl of grapes while you wait. He should be along any minute."

He'd been so smug about the fact that she never caught on, but looking back, he was embarrassed to realize she must have known what he was doing. He'd looked like a damn scarecrow in ill-fitting clothes that needed patching, shooting up in height faster than he could pack a pound on his scrawny frame.

Donna was wrong. His dedication to making people like him wasn't "pathological." It was strategic. He'd relied on the gifts he had to survive and get ahead. He wasn't going to apologize for his calculating nature, either.

So he won over people—how was that hurting anyone? It wasn't as if he was using his skills to con others out of money or deceive them.

Armed with that solid rationalization, he made a bee-line for Grace's van. She was already in the backseat with Antonio, which didn't leave much room for Ty. He ended up in the middle row between Phoebe and heavily freck-led Stuart Capriotti. The other passengers were from the show's crew.

Phoebe wagged her finger at Ty. "I hope you and Grace are planning to go easy on the rest of us today. We have plenty of time before the final winner is chosen—give someone else a chance to look good, too!"

"I never go easy on anyone. But I'll say this." He flashed her a smile. "You don't need me to make you look good. You do that all by yourself."

She preened. "Flatterer."

While he was trying to decide the best way to engage Grace in conversation, Phoebe asked if he knew what he was making. He had narrowed his "perfect bite" to two options, depending on the availability and quality of in-gredients in the store, but he had no intention of giving information to his competitors. Instead he made a non-committal noise and volleyed back the question. "What about you, Phoebe?"

Unsurprisingly the pastry chef was sticking with her dessert background. "Crème-filled, chocolate-dipped macaroons." She exhaled a breathy sigh. "They're *divine.* Come by my station later, and I'll let you try one." As if belatedly remembering they weren't alone, Phoebe added, "That goes for the rest of you, too. If you've got a sweet tooth, I'm your gal."

On Ty's other side, Stuart raised a red eyebrow. "Gen-erous offer, Phoebe, but do you think it's wise to tell us what you're planning before the shopping's done? What if it gives us a tactical advantage?"

"Don't be silly," Phoebe said. "None of you are known for desserts. It would be ridiculous to switch your idea just because of what I'm doing. Right, Grace? Chime in and defend me. We ladies have to stick together."

"Sure thing," Grace said flatly. "Girl power. All the way."

"Huh." Phoebe swiveled her head to shoot a disappointed look at the only other female contestant in the van. "Your cooking must be more passionate than your feminism, or there's no way you would have won yesterday. Unless Ty did all the heavy lifting." She tittered, giving her words that I'm-joking-no-I'm-not feel.

"I run my own restaurant." Grace punctuated her statement with a glare hot enough to sear tuna steaks. "I don't need anyone to do my 'lifting' for me."

Ty entertained fantasies of smacking Phoebe upside the head. Here he was trying to do damage control for last night, and the blonde was further irritating Grace. Then again, maybe the pastry chef had given him the exact opening he needed.

"Have you been to Grace's restaurant?" he asked Phoebe. "The Twisted Jalapeño. I haven't had the pleasure of actually eating an entire meal, but my manager and I stopped in for appetizers the other night. Best salsa verde I've ever had."

He used the rearview mirror to peek back at Grace and see if his words had diminished her ire. Nope. Eyes narrowed, she looked irritated *and* suspicious.

"It was my father's recipe," she said, dismissing his compliment. "I can't take credit."

Unlike Phoebe, Grace was clearly not a woman to be placated with flattery. Rather than make any more missteps, Ty listened patiently while Grace and Antonio fell into discussion about her dad. A few minutes later, they arrived at the specialty grocery store. Ty exited the van and let Phoebe, Stuart and the cameraman get ahead of him while Ty lingered behind, waiting for Grace.

She did a hilariously poor job of pretending to ignore him as she climbed down. If she wanted to give him the brush-off, she should try harder to look composed. Cold shoulder was not in her repertoire; Grace burned too hot for that. Her eyes were like dark fireworks, her anger at him glinting for the whole world to see. Tension ricocheted off her body.

"Grace, wait." He reached lightly for her arm, nodding briefly to Antonio, grateful when the older man moved past them. "I just wanted to ask if your visit went okay this morning. With, um, your mom," he clarified needlessly.

Stupid. Where was his trademark glib tongue? He felt clunky and inarticulate, like someone trying to give a speech with a mouthful of Novocain.

Grace looked startled by his question but quickly regrouped to answer. The frown lines across her forehead even smoothed, giving him reason to believe her morning hadn't been too difficult after all. Good. He was genuinely happy for her.

But then she scowled again. "We're on a tight schedule, Beckett, and I need to get in the store. I don't have time for 'a big sharing session' about my family." After lobbing his own words back at him, she pivoted and walked away.

So much for damage control.

GRACE SLAMMED THE FRONT door, wincing at the echo and her own foul mood. *I should be ecstatic.* Although it was taking some time, her mother seemed to be settling into her new home, and, after today's performance, Grace had established herself as an early favorite in this all-important cooking competition.

"Grace?" Amy's voice drifted from her room. "Is that you, or were we hit by a very brief earthquake?" The bartender shuffled into the living room at the front of the tiny house. "A picture fell off my wall. Books plummeted from shelves."

Grace ducked her head guiltily. "Sorry."

"No apology necessary. I was just trying to decide whether to spend the rest of the evening huddled in a doorway waiting for the aftershocks."

Grace managed a tired laugh. "Well, if that's how you *want* to spend your night off, I won't stop you."

"So what gives, *chica?*" Amy's face suddenly paled. "You're not out of the running for most badass chef? That can't be it. Tell me that's not it!"

"No. I got second place this afternoon. And coming in right behind Katharine Garner isn't exactly something to be ashamed of." If the words came out sounding like flat recitation, it was because she'd been telling herself that same thing for the entire drive home. *Don't think of it as losing ground just because you slipped a place. Look at it like the Olympics—one of your culinary idols took gold and you joined her on the podium with silver.* Which would make Ty, with his combination of spicy grilled green bean bundles and dry white wine spritzer, the bronze medalist.

Amy let out a whoop, gyrating in an impromptu happy dance. "First and second in forty-eight hours? You are on a roll!" She stopped wiggling her hips. "So why were you trying to tear our front door off its hinges? There are easier ways to remodel."

"I said I was sorry," Grace muttered, heading for the kitchen by force of habit even though she wasn't remotely hungry. She didn't even feel like cooking.

She hoisted herself onto one of the bar stools and propped her elbows on the counter. "Guess I'm just frazzled by the pressure."

"After two challenges? Pace yourself," Amy cautioned.

"Maybe not the pressure, so much as…"

Amy sat on the other stool. "Yes?"

"The other contestants." Specifically Ty Beckett. And possibly Phoebe Verlaine, although it felt catty to think badly of someone who'd been eliminated from the contest. The blonde had burst into tears when the judges informed her she'd lost.

It had seemed a unanimous decision that her pairing was a failure. She'd been scolded for her portion size, which was far more than a typical *amuse-bouche* mouthful, as well as the texture of her macaroons and her choice of a too-sweet dessert wine that overamplified the chocolate instead of underscoring it. Grace, who'd been praised for her mussels cooked in coconut milk and topped with supreme of lime served with an awesome gimlet, had felt real pity for the sobbing pastry chef.

Some of that sympathy had faded, however, when a tearful Phoebe had turned to Ty for solace, burying her face in his chest. The scene reminded Grace far too much of when she'd become emotional during their dart game and Ty had pulled her into his arms. She'd been foolish enough to think that—

"Grace? You're scaring me," Amy said.

"What? I wasn't doing anything."

"Maybe not, but you should see the look on your face. It's a little homicidal. Like I should worry about you breaking through the door of my room with an ax one night, saying, 'Heeere's Gracie.'"

"Anyone ever mention you have a truly warped imagination?"

"Don't change the subject. You were telling me which one of the other chefs has you upset. And I'll bet I know exactly who you were going to say. Ty Beckett." Amy's eyes widened as she studied her roommate, then she snapped her fingers. "Aha! I knew it."

Grace pressed her hands to her heated cheeks. Crap, her brothers were right. She really had no semblance of a poker face. For form's sake, she attempted a bluff anyway. "There goes your wacky imagination again."

Amy shook her head. "Even last night, I knew something was up."

It had been late when Amy got home from the restaurant, and Grace had just finished showering and dressing for bed. She'd informed Amy that she and Ty had won their team challenge—and had gone out for a quick bite to celebrate afterward—but when Amy had pressed for details, Grace pleaded an early morning and retreated.

"You should have been more excited about your win," Amy said. "Normally you get all keyed-up about good news and can't stop chatting. It was weird how you disappeared into your room without answering any of my questions. What happened?"

Grace bit her lip. Would rehashing everything make her feel better or worse? "Ty Beckett's not at all what I expected. Except, in some ways, he's *exactly* what I expected."

Amy blinked. "You have some kind of decoder ring to go with that explanation?"

"Never mind. I'm just making a big deal out of nothing. He was nice yesterday—a little bossy and too used to getting his own way, but basically nice. And actually kind of great last night. Until right at the end, I inadvertently put my foot in my mouth by asking about his family, which is apparently forbidden." *Even though I told him all about mine.* "It was awkward for a few minutes, but then I dropped him off at his hotel. Case closed."

"So why are you slamming doors with the wrath of a thousand scorned women?"

She exhaled in a huff. "I don't know. He kind of got under my skin this morning, and then there was this other chef, Phoebe. She hinted that maybe the reason I won yesterday was because of my partner's talent, and I spent all day sort of wanting to stab her with a shrimp fork. But then she got eliminated, which made me feel bad for her. Until she threw herself at Ty."

Amy grinned knowingly. "Which made you want to stab both of them?"

"It's not like that. I'm not interested in him. It just made me wonder if he's the type to exploit a woman's vulnerabilities." Assuming that Phoebe's tears had been real and not a manufactured ploy. *Maybe they deserve each other.* "I…let my guard down last night, talked a little about Mom."

She recalled the way he'd teased her, telling her he wasn't sweet at all, that he'd just seized the excuse to hold "a beautiful woman." What if he hadn't been kidding? What if that really was his M.O.? Not that his dating life mattered to her, but, in retrospect, she felt foolish for thinking there'd been some connection between them.

Grace slid off her stool, too frustrated to sit still any longer. "This morning, he had the nerve to ask about my breakfast with Mom, and I don't know what to think. It could mean he was considerate enough to be worried about it. Or that it was a mind game, bringing up something personal right before the challenge to disconcert me. I guess that's what has me so cranky. I can't tell if he's a great guy or possibly the devil."

Following suit, Amy stood. "I don't know what to say. A lot of women have made the mistake of thinking a slimeball is a prince, yet other women are too paranoid to give honestly decent guys a chance. It's the type of decision best gauged after the fact…which does nothing to help you right now. However, living with a bartender does have certain useful perks. Want to try out some new drink ideas I have for the Jalapeño?"

"Maybe later," Grace said. "I didn't sleep well last night, and half my problem is probably exhaustion. Even half a drink might knock me into a coma."

"So take tomorrow to rest," Amy suggested. "You said there's no filming on Wednesday, right?"

"No challenge," Grace clarified. "They're shooting some footage of the area and doing behind-the-scenes interviews with some of the chefs. I had mine tonight, which means I get to spend tomorrow at the restaurant." *Hallelujah.*

As appreciative as she was for the opportunity of this competition, she was thrilled to have twenty-four hours where she'd be free of it—and of Ty Beckett.

"OH, IT'S GOOD TO BE BACK!" Grace sang out. Her voice echoed through the empty restaurant.

Nearly empty, anyway. "Grace?" Victor poked his head out of the office, wearing the suit and tie required for his bank job. No doubt he would be headed there in the next half hour or so.

He greeted her with an absent smile, looking confused. "What are you doing here this early? And why do you sound so happy about it? I thought you were a night person by nature."

"I'm just glad to have the day to myself." She leaned against the wall, trying not to notice the places where the paint was chipping. "A return to real life. This TV thing—"

"Is it putting too much stress on you?" he interrupted. "Because you don't *have* to do this. I feel like you're throwing yourself on the grenade, taking it as your responsibility to save the restaurant for all of us. You don't owe us that. You're allowed to have a life."

This place *was* her life. But she was afraid saying so would only make him worry more.

"I had breakfast with Mom yesterday," she said, clumsily changing the subject. "She seems like she's doing better. Speaking of breakfast, have you eaten yet? I could make us something." She straightened, glancing eagerly toward the kitchen.

Victor checked his watch. "Thanks, but I can't stay much longer. I only came in to update some accounting software on the computer before I go to work. Maybe after the bank closes this afternoon, I'll go see Mom, too. Except for our Sunday dinners, I haven't visited her nearly as often as I should."

Indecision snaked through her. Did he know Natalie had been visiting? Should Grace warn him about their mother's wild idea that Nat and Vic were expecting?

"Um, Victor." She cleared her throat, studying the tops of his shoes. He kept them impressively shiny.

"Jeez. You look like you did when you were sixteen, trying to figure out how to tell Dad about the dent in the sedan. How worried should I be?"

"Not worried," she hastily assured him. "Still, it couldn't hurt to sit down." She steered him into the office, but kept stalling once they got there. *Coffee is not stalling. Coffee is a biological necessity.*

"Seriously," Victor said from behind her, "did you side-swipe my car in the parking lot?"

She laughed. "Even as an uneasy sixteen-year-old driver, I think I could have avoided hitting the only other car in a deserted lot. No, this is about Mom."

He sat forward, instantly alert. "You said she was doing better."

"As far as adjusting to her living arrangements, she definitely is! But she still has Alzheimer's. She's going to get confused at times." Grace hesitated. "I'm not sure she remembers you and Natalie are separated."

Pain glazed his eyes, but he managed to keep it out of his voice. Both her brothers were far better at suppressing emotions than she'd ever be. If Victor were more in touch with his feelings, could he have convinced his wife he loved her enough to keep working on their marriage?

Grace continued softly. "Mom mentioned that Natalie had been by and looked tired, not quite herself. She—Mom—got it into her head that maybe Natalie was pregnant."

Victor exhaled in a surprised *whoosh.* "Pregnant? That's the most ridiculous thing I've ever heard."

"It's possible Mom will forget all about it by the time you talk to her. But I thought you should know, just in case."

Victor had shot out of his chair and was pacing, even though the office didn't actually provide enough room for that. They'd both inherited the tendency to pace from their father; Ben was the only one of the three of them who could keep still. He was focused and endlessly patient. It made him the best in the family at fishing and, Grace assumed, helped him take down criminals.

"I shouldn't have told you before work." Grace second-guessed herself. "Now you're upset."

"Graciela, I've been 'upset' since my crazy wife told me she didn't want to be married anymore!" He tossed his hands in the air. "Anything else that happens now is just another raindrop in the ocean."

She sat on the edge of the desk, trying to give him more room. "I don't get it," she admitted. "You guys didn't fight much, and neither of you is interested in anyone else." Though Victor had never dated as many girls as his younger brother, when he had been in a relationship, he'd been a model boyfriend. Good with numbers, he *always* remembered birthdays and anniversaries. Though the most introverted of the three Torres siblings, he wasn't cold.

"She told me I was sucking the joy out of her life." His voice was ragged, more hurt than Grace had heard him sound since their father died. "Can you imagine what it feels like for your spouse, your other half, to say that to you? I've been a damn good husband. I don't think there's anything else I can do, so maybe she's right. She should go find joy elsewhere."

And what about you? Grace ached for her brother. How long would it be until he discovered happiness again?

Victor shook his head. "Maybe you're right not to make romance a priority. It has a way of biting you on the ass."

"Not for everyone," she objected, thinking of their parents. When they'd disagreed, Colleen and Victor Senior had argued loudly and passionately, but no one ever questioned how devoted they were to each other and their family. They'd taken life side by side, each the other's biggest fan and supporter. Whatever dream one had attempted, the other had cheered and helped make reality.

While her brother was right that dating didn't currently

take precedence in Grace's life, if she discovered someone who could love her as unreservedly as her mother and father had loved each other, she'd shift her priorities. Could Victor take hope in the memories of their parents, in the possibility that he'd still find that kind of connection, or would bringing up their parents' enviable relationship only make him feel like more of a failure? Before she could decide what to say, the phone rang.

Victor's eyebrows lifted. "Seems too early for calls on the restaurant line."

She was already diving for the phone, knowing the machine would pick up after the second ring. "Hello? This is Grace Torres speaking."

"Just the gal I was hopin' to reach," the man on the other end of the phone drawled.

She smiled fondly at Sam Travis's voice. "How's my favorite cowboy doing?" She hadn't spoken to him much since his landlady, Wanda Keller, died. Though stoic Sam kept his emotions even closer to the vest than Victor, Grace knew Sam had cared about the elderly woman.

"I was actually callin' to see how your restaurant's doin'," he deflected. "Still need help with some repairs? I finished a job at one of the ranches sooner than expected and won't start festival setup until tomorrow." He hesitated, then admitted, "I need to get out. Some days, it's tough to be here."

Until the festival was over, Sam was staying at the bed-and-breakfast where Wanda had kept a permanent room for him. Although Sam and Wanda hadn't been related by blood, she'd been like a mother figure to him. Grace recalled just how difficult it had been to be at the Jalapeño immediately following her dad's death.

"Today would be a perfect day to tackle some repairs," Grace declared. She squirmed under the weight of Victor's sudden frown. "Although, technically, repair work might not be in this month's budget."

"Pay me in free appetizers," Sam suggested.

Grace laughed. "That's not fair to you. Aren't you moving on to a job in Burnet soon?"

"Well, wherever I hang my hat next, trust me, your cooking would be worth the drive."

"SAM? SAM…SAM!" GRACE finally raised her voice to get the man to glance down from his position on the ladder. *Okay, I know I'm short, but there's no way I'm too low to the ground for him to hear me.* As grateful as she was for his maintenance assistance, she had to admit he was uncharacteristically preoccupied.

His distraction could be attributed to any one of a hundred things. Yet Grace couldn't help thinking of the rumors she'd heard that he was staying in the bed-and-breakfast alone with Wanda's daughter, a woman named Lorelei who'd come home to Texas for her mother's memorial service. Grace had asked him about Lorelei when he'd arrived earlier and, although it was difficult to tell under Sam's year-round tan, for a second, she could have sworn he reddened.

He looked embarrassed again now, regarding her expectantly from above.

"I really appreciate everything you've done," she told him, "but we open for dinner in a couple of hours."

"Be right down," he promised. "This was the last bulb."

She glanced around and gave a rueful shake of her head. "Considering some of the cracked booth seats and broken tiles, maybe I shouldn't have added more light. Dim might be better for ambience."

He descended onto the floor next to her. "Grace, your

enchiladas would be delicious even if guests had to sit in the dark on three-legged chairs."

She laughed, wondering if he'd ever consider a career as a restaurant critic. He had an unusual but effective way with words. She just hoped the competition judges ultimately shared Sam's high opinion of her food.

As evening staff began trickling in to prepare for the night ahead, Sam gathered his tools and placed Wet Paint signs in the necessary areas. When he was finished, Grace rushed to head him off at the door. She had a sneaking suspicion he might "forget" to accept his payment before leaving.

"Thank you again." She thrust an envelope of cash toward him, knowing he'd quoted her far less than his time and talent were worth. It was a shame Sam's trail rides and seasonal ranch jobs kept him on the move rather than in Fredericksburg long-term; he was a good guy. Unexpectedly her mind flashed to Ty and the way he never seemed to remain in one place, either. The corner of her lips twitched. Maybe Ty was a culinary cowboy.

Sam glanced at the envelope, and for a second she thought he might refuse it. Her pride shrieked for him to take the money. She didn't mind a discount between friends, but the thought of outright charity chafed. It made the Jalapeño seem even less like the thriving eatery she remembered from her childhood.

Finally he took the envelope, offering her a slight nod.

She sighed in mingled relief and wistfulness. "I just wish I could afford bigger changes instead of small patch jobs."

"Hang in there," he advised. "Once you win that hotshot competition, you might be able to fix the place up more."

"From your lips to God's ears," she said. Heaven only knew what cooking challenge tomorrow would bring.

But for tonight, she had a restaurant to run.

It was ironic that Ty had spent Wednesday afternoon being asked questions about himself and hadn't discussed the one topic that was actually meaningful. When interviewed about what he would be doing once the competition was over, he'd given vague, cagey responses that alluded to his own cooking show without saying anything specific about the unsolidified deal. But he hadn't mentioned the charity foundation he and Stephen were setting in motion. Some celebrities used the media to get the word out about causes that were close to their hearts, but feeding hungry kids was a bit *too* close for Ty's comfort.

So he kept his answers light and entertaining. After the interviews were all concluded, he shared a van ride back to the inn with red-haired Stuart Capriotti and molecular gastronomist Reed Lockhart, whom the other chefs had nicknamed "Mr. Science." No sooner had the three men set foot inside the hotel lobby than he heard his name called by Phoebe Verlaine.

"Ty!"

I thought she was gone already. He knew the producers had paid for her to stay one final night in Fredericksburg after her elimination, but Ty had assumed she'd left hours ago.

"Hey, Phoebe." He conjured a smile for her benefit, but, truthfully, he wasn't all that happy to see her. The woman was reputed to be a great pastry chef—poor performance in this competition notwithstanding—and she was undeniably pretty. But he was beginning to find her cloying. She stood too close, said his name too often.

Give her a break. When had he become so cranky?

Attractive women flirting with him had never bothered him before now. Maybe it wasn't Phoebe's fault. Next to the daggers he was getting from Grace Torres, a woman so much as smiling in his direction would seem forward in contrast.

"I didn't realize you'd still be here," he told Phoebe. "Does this mean we get the pleasure of your company a little longer?"

She shook her head, blond curls bouncing around her face. "Afraid not. I left my bags with the people at the front desk while I did some sightseeing today, but now I'm headed out for real. I'm sorry I didn't get to see more of you, though. I'd hoped that you and I could…work together."

"Maybe another time." The words came out automatically, testament to his policy of never burning bridges and always leaving a good final impression. *Almost* always. He frowned at the memory of Grace's scathing sarcasm when he'd tried to make peace yesterday.

The good news was, he planned to be in town for the duration of this competition. He had plenty of time to improve her opinion of him.

"Ty?" Phoebe leaned forward, laying her hand across his chest. "I was just thinking, you made Grace's restaurant sound so wonderful when you talked about it. If you don't already have dinner plans, maybe you could show it to me? I have time for a quick bite on my way out of town."

Dinner with Phoebe? The suggestion caught him off guard, though it wasn't as if she'd been particularly subtle about her interest in him. In theory, he liked bold women. But this attraction was awkwardly one-sided—Ty's attentions lay elsewhere.

In cooking. That's where my focus is—cook circles

around everyone else, win this contest, secure your show.
When he finally reached that level of success, he would
relax. He could celebrate by taking out a different blonde
every night! Although, come to think of it, maybe he was
more partial to brunettes.

"So, how 'bout it?" Phoebe purred. "You, me, dinner?"

"Sure. Guess I just don't have the willpower to stay
away from that salsa verde." Or the feisty, voluptuous chef
who made it.

Chapter Six

This is exactly what I needed. Grace was in her element at the Jalapeño. Not only did she love overseeing activity in the kitchen, but she'd enjoyed the earlier break she'd taken to mingle with patrons. Her brother Ben—upgraded from his wheelchair to crutches—had come in with Zane Winchester, a Texas Ranger who sometimes assisted local law enforcement, and Zane's teenage daughter. Grace didn't know much about the Winchesters except that Zane had only recently gained custody of his daughter; the sullen girl was clearly not pleased about moving to Fredericksburg. It had warmed Grace's heart to watch the teen drop her indifferent facade and enthusiastically dig into a serving of slow-cooked pork and peppers.

Grace's dad had been of the belief that almost all problems could be solved with great food. He'd harbored a theory that if world leaders could sit around the table for a truly kick-ass meal together, maybe there'd be peace. Colleen had chided him for saying "kick-ass" in front of their daughter, and shortly thereafter he'd started teaching Grace to swear in Spanish—not that they'd ever fooled Colleen by resorting to a different language.

"Got an order for a VIP!" Angela, their newest waitress, breezed into the kitchen. "That hunky Sam Travis is here."

"He is?" Grace looked up from the batch of cucumber-wasabi salsa she was making. "He only left a couple of hours ago."

"Well, he's back." Angela heaved a sigh. "With a date."

"You're kidding!"

"Wish I were." It was no secret that Angela was one of a dozen women in town half in love with Sam.

Grace racked her brain but couldn't remember him ever bringing a date here. Who was he with, and what was she like? Curiosity bubbled over like milk at full boil, but one of the waiters came in with an order for a large party that required Grace's attention. Once the entrées were being plated and a batch of black bean brownies were in the oven, Grace decided she could afford a five-minute break to see Sam's mystery woman for herself.

But it wasn't the woman Grace noticed first as she approached the table—it was Sam and how different he looked. He was wearing one of his regular jeans and dark T-shirt combinations, just as she'd seen him a hundred times, but his expression was unfamiliar. He was leaning toward the beautiful brunette across the table from him, and his gaze… Well, the only adjective Grace could think of was "softer" but that made him sound less masculine when the opposite was true. Although there was an air of vulnerability she'd never witnessed in him, he also seemed fiercely male, completely attuned to and protective of the woman with him.

If a guy looked at Grace like that, she'd melt like a pat of butter on a sizzling skillet. Recalling the moment that afternoon when she'd had to call Sam's name three times just to get his attention, Grace knew without a doubt that his dinner companion was the reason why. *He's got it bad.*

Suddenly Grace realized she was standing still, staring rudely at two of her guests. Embarrassed, she cleared her throat and propelled herself forward. "Sam!"

He favored her with a huge smile in greeting. "Grace, dinner's wonderful as usual. And you've made a new convert tonight." He turned back to the woman he'd been watching with such rapt attention. "Grace Torres, meet Lorelei Keller."

"Wanda Keller's daughter?" So this was the infamous Lorelei from up north? Manners overrode Grace's curiosity. "I'm so very sorry for your loss. She was a lovely woman. She often visited my aunt in the nursing home and listened to her spin tales, like the time *Tía* Maria swears she encountered *la llorona*."

Wanda had collected folk tales, and telling stories was one of Maria's talents that had only improved with age.

Lorelei had cocked her head to the side, looking confused, so Sam offered a quick explanation for *la llorona*. "The weeping woman, a figure in Hispanic folklore."

Grace nodded. "*Mi tía* looked forward to those afternoons. Your mother will be greatly missed. Dinner is on the house for you two!" The gesture was prompted not only from respect for Wanda's memory but gratitude. Seeing the way Sam and Lorelei were looking at each other had reminded Grace of her own parents. She was thankful to be reminded that people could still find that bond.

But Lorelei protested. "Oh, let us pay! Please."

"Out of the question. Your money is no good here." Of course, given the current state of their books, Victor would have a stroke if he heard her giving away free food. "Not tonight, anyway. But you'll come again soon, yes?"

"Definitely," Lorelei agreed. "I was already planning to return while I'm in town."

"Will you be here long?" Grace had temporarily forgotten that Sam himself would be leaving after the festival. What would happen to that indefinable gleam in his eye when he and Lorelei had gone their separate ways?

"Only another week or so," Lorelei replied. "But I may have to come back once or twice before the inn's final sale."

"You're not keeping it?" Grace had subconsciously assumed Lorelei would run the inn now that Wanda was gone. "Taking over the family business?"

"Mom didn't buy the inn until after I'd moved away for college," Lorelei explained with a shrug. "I don't really see it as the family business."

For a horribly guilty moment, Grace envied the other woman. She wasn't burdened with keeping the establishment open and profitable. She wouldn't feel like a failure, or as if she'd lost her mother all over again, when the place passed into new hands.

"Understandable," she mumbled to Lorelei. "Well, good luck finding new owners and you two enjoy the rest of your meal."

As she backed away from the table, tears blurred her vision. She was ashamed that she'd been jealous, even temporarily, of Lorelei's freedom. The Jalapeño had been a gift from her family, the two Torres generations who'd come before her, and it was a gift she wanted to share with the community. It wasn't a burden! But voices collided in her head, Victor telling her she didn't have to throw herself on the grenade, Ty enumerating how much responsibility a restaurant was. He'd told her he didn't think he should have to apologize for having fun, and he was right.

With a deep sigh, she promised herself she'd have fun when the Jalapeño was solvent.

As she turned toward the kitchen, she caught a glance of Rosie the hostess ushering a couple to a romantically lit dim booth in the far corner of the dining room. Grace started in surprise. *Ty?* She shook her head. Was he really so much on her mind that she was seeing him in random men? While the man on the other side of the restaurant did have a similar build and hair color, she'd only glimpsed him from the back. If he turned around, he probably wouldn't resemble Ty at all.

More pressing than the man's identity was the fact that she was letting herself get distracted. Today had been the first day all week when she'd been free to forget about Ty Beckett, and she was dismayed to find that she hadn't. He'd been sneaking in and out of her thoughts like a cat burglar. It was demoralizing. The man would gloat mercilessly if he knew he'd gotten under her skin.

She detoured in the direction of the bar, wanting a glass of ice water and the diversion of Amy's chatter. But tonight, most of the seats at the bar were actually full. Grace waited patiently, glad to see her roommate filling so many drinks and convincing people to try the house chili-lime margarita. A respectable dinner crowd had formed. Although most festival tourists wouldn't arrive for another day or so, regional vendors who were participating had begun trickling into town. There were temporary pavilions to set up and booths to be prepared.

Normally out-of-towners ended up at some of the better-publicized restaurants, but even with *Road Trip* just starting to get under way, she'd noticed increased interest in the Jalapeño. A couple of diners had told her they were proud she was representing Fredericksburg; irrepressibly cheerful Tess Fitzpatrick, a local dance teacher and Jalapeño regular, had asked with a conspiratorial smile if Ty Beckett was as hot in person as he was on TV.

Grace hadn't volunteered an opinion, instead joking that Tess should come to some of the scheduled cooking demonstrations at the festival and decide for herself. But truthfully, the man was far more devastating in person. A camera might pick up the glint in his eye, but when he was actually with you and—

"Grace!"

She jumped, pressing a hand against her racing heart as if the pressure would slow her pulse. "Jeez, Amy. You scared the life out of me."

"You didn't hear me the first two times?" Her friend eyed her quizzically.

Grace's face flamed. "My, um, mind must've been elsewhere."

"Well, now that I've got your attention." Amy leaned as far forward as she could with the bar between them, lowering her voice to a stage whisper. "In case you didn't know already, I thought you would appreciate the headsup. Have you seen who's at table twelve?"

Grace groaned. "Don't tell me." Apparently he *hadn't* been an optical illusion produced by too much Ty on the brain.

Funny, but she would have thought she'd be more relieved by that.

ANGELA CAME INTO THE kitchen fanning herself with her hand. "And I thought Sam was good-looking! Ty Beckett more than gives him a run for his money."

Grace indulged herself in mentally firing the woman. Out loud, she only said, "If you like that type."

Angela gaped. "Are you telling me there's a woman who *doesn't?* He asked for you, by the way. He and his date want to pay their compliments."

Grace clenched her jaw. Why was he pursuing her? She'd been perfectly happy to work in the kitchen for the past hour and ignore him. Far be it from her to ruin his romantic evening with whichever admirer he'd taken to dinner. But here he was, cornering her in her own restaurant.

She'd made it clear yesterday that she had nothing to say to him and wanted to be left alone. So why was he here? Was it an ego thing? Was he simply too unused to the rejection? Some choice phrases came to mind regarding his overblown sense of self-worth, but she bit her tongue. She wasn't about to let him goad her in front of her customers.

You can do this. Go out there, be brief, be gracious, then tell him you have work to do. Which he would better understand if he ever attempted to run a restaurant, but heaven forbid he invested that much effort into anything.

Halfway to table twelve, Grace's step faltered as she realized who was seated with Ty. At the sight of Phoebe simpering at him, Grace couldn't help glancing around the dining room to see if Ben was still here. She wanted to borrow one of his crutches just long enough to smack Ty on the head.

"Ty, Phoebe," she grated. It wasn't exactly the welcoming tone she'd hoped to achieve. "What an unexpected surprise."

Ty grinned at her, those silvery eyes mocking. "As opposed to an *expected* surprise?"

Phoebe tittered, and Grace had to stop herself from adding that the reason she was so surprised was that she'd expected Phoebe to slink out of town after her resounding elimination yesterday. *Be the better woman, Gracie.* "I hope the two of you enjoyed your dinners." *And will be leaving soon. Don't let the door hit you in the butt.*

"It was all right," Phoebe allowed, her previous smirk fading.

"All right?" Ty echoed dubiously. "It was fantastic. I

inhaled my spicy lamb burrito, then finished off the rest of Phoebe's blue-corn crepes."

Aw, how sweet—they'd shared each other's food. Her smile tightened across her cheeks like that mud mask facial she'd had when Amy gave her a spa gift certificate for her birthday. She could feel little cracks forming in her expression.

"Glad everything was to your liking, but duty calls. If you'll excuse me, I'll leave you two to the rest of your… night." She turned without waiting for a response. But of course, he wouldn't let her get away that easily. Moments later, she heard Ty's voice behind her.

"You got a second?"

She closed her eyes, her resolve to remain professional faltering. She wanted to grab him by the collar of his shirt and shake him. Afraid he was brazen enough to follow her into the kitchen, where the staff would eavesdrop unabashedly, she angled into an alcove where there'd once been a pay phone, before the days when everyone had a cell. It was about as private as they could get under current circumstances.

She whirled around. "You know, I wasn't kidding about duty calling. I have an actual job to do."

He nodded, his eyes earnest. "I can see that. The restaurant's really hopping tonight!" His voice was so encouraging it almost veered into condescension. It reminded her of the time she'd gotten that ill-advised perm and Ben had chirped as soon as he saw her that, in case he'd never mentioned it, she had *really* pretty eyes.

"I know how much this place means to you," Ty said. "Must be a relief to see it so packed."

If she had any kind of guarantee business would keep up like this *after* the festival, she could breathe again. "Stop it."

"Stop what?"

"Everything! Stop following me. Stop trying to befriend me. Stop pretending like you care." This conversation was as bad as when he'd asked about her mom with such concern in his eyes. He turned that sincerity on and off so easily.

He had the nerve to look taken aback. "I wasn't pretending. And I was serious about the food being great, not that you can take a compliment. I've known cacti less prickly than you."

"You don't know me. If you did, you'd understand I'm about the long-term, things that last. Family, community, friends that have my undying loyalty. I don't do superficial relationships where two people share a fake bond for a couple of hours and then move on to the next shallow encounter." She'd meant to refer to their game of darts—when she'd mistakenly confided in him only to regret it later—but her gaze flickered back to table twelve, where Phoebe glared at them with palpable impatience.

Ty looked over his shoulder. "Are you mad because I'm here with her?"

"I don't care who you date," she insisted. "But if I stopped long enough to form an opinion, I'd probably think you two are a perfect match. All syrupy sweetness and no substance. Just try not to give each other cavities."

EVEN THOUGH HE'D BEEN THE one to give the cabbie this location, Ty was almost surprised to find himself at the bar—the same one he and Grace had come to a couple of nights ago. Why was he back? *Too restless to call it an evening.* He wondered if, when Phoebe had proposed they go to the Jalapeño, she'd envisioned driving him back to the hotel afterward and perhaps being invited to his room.

He'd been spared having to rebuff her tactfully. By the

time he'd returned to their table, Phoebe had informed him she wanted to hit the road before it got any later and icily suggested he grab a taxi back to the hotel. He'd come here instead.

After ordering a drink, he chose a table in the back and halfheartedly watched a basketball game playing on the big screen above the bar. Grace's words churned inside him, leaving him mildly nauseous, as if he'd mixed one too many flavors that didn't go together. She saw him as shallow and self-absorbed, throwing friends and family in his face.

Big talk from a woman who'd had two parents who adored her and a couple of older brothers. She didn't know the first damn thing about being an only child whose family had consisted solely of one half-interested parent. Beth had cared about him in a vague, preoccupied-with-her-own-problems kind of way, but she'd barely been more than a child herself.

A man couldn't choose his family. *I have friends, though.* People loved him. He could build his own community; they didn't have to be in one central location. Friendships weren't confined to town limits. But even as he mentally rattled off a list of friends, he admitted to himself that most of the names fell into two categories— professional acquaintances and former lovers.

There was Stephen, who probably knew him better than anyone else, but Stephen might not count. After all, he was *paid* to put up with Ty.

Ty pulled out his cell phone and dialed.

Stephen answered immediately. "Hello?"

"Am I superficial and selfish?" Ty asked without preamble.

"Yes. Can I go back to watching TV with my wife now?"

"Sure. Sorry to bother you."

"Wait, were you serious? Honey—I mean Donna, not you."

"Figured."

Stephen's voice was muffled as he turned away from the phone. "Honey, can you pause this a minute? It's Ty. He's having some kind of thing."

"It's not a thing," Ty said defensively. "It was just a question. And I don't even know why I asked. It's not like she—"

"She?" Stephen pounced. "This is about Chef Torres, isn't it? Man, I warned you she was your kryptonite!"

"You're full of it." Ty rocked his chair back on two legs, staring idly at the television as a player shot a beautiful free throw. "Don't you remember my email saying Grace and I won the first challenge together? How is that kryptonite?"

"Yet you don't sound like you're calling to tell me about another win. What's up?"

"Nothing. I mean, it's a contest. Someone's going to win, lots of other people are going to lose, and that's going to generate some tension, right? It's inevitable."

"So you're experiencing tension with all of the opponents, then." Stephen paused before asking slyly, "Or just one in particular?"

"You're a pain in the ass. I don't know why I called you."

Stephen laughed. "Because I give it to you straight and because you can't bullshit me. I'm not blinded by the Ty Beckett megawatt smile and salesman personality."

"Our third challenge starts tomorrow," Ty said. "I'll text you and let you know how it goes."

"Hold on a sec." There was indistinct conversation as

Stephen and his wife talked. Then he was back. "Donna wanted me to tell you to kick some ass."

"I always do."

Moments after Ty ended the call, he also finished his drink. He didn't particularly want another, but he didn't want to go back to his hotel room, either. When he was there, it was too easy to picture Grace pacing back and forth in front of the bed, arguing spiritedly.

Thoughts of Grace, combined with his general edginess tonight, led him toward the section where the dartboards hung. On the way, he passed a man whose scowl was as black as his cowboy hat.

Ty cleared his throat. "Any interest in a game of darts?" At least trying to aim would give him something to dwell on besides how he kept managing to put his foot in his mouth where Grace was concerned. He'd been on his best behavior tonight! His praise of her food had been completely genuine, and he'd thought making small talk about how well her restaurant was doing was a can't-miss. It seemed like a sure topic to put her in a good mood. Yet she'd bristled so defensively one would think he'd said her pants made her look too wide through the hips. A preposterous hypothetical—Grace's hips were perfect. Why didn't she ever give him the benefit of the doubt?

Infuriating woman.

The man in the cowboy hat stood. "Darts, huh? Why not?" He held out his hand. "Name's Sam."

"Ty."

The two of them progressed to the closest dartboard and agreed on a game of Oh-One. Considering his luck at darts the other night, Ty was glad Sam didn't suggest playing for money. After a few rounds, though, Ty realized he might have actually stood a chance. Sam had thrown several wild shots and seemed so annoyed with his performance that he was making some sort of low growling sound in the back of his throat.

Not that I'm doing much better. Ty stepped forward to throw but instead of the board, he kept seeing Grace's face. Smiling as she joked with him the other night, hurt when she'd dropped him off at his hotel, flashing fire tonight when she'd told him to leave her alone. Why was that turning out to be so much easier said than done? Was Donna right—did he have some neurotic need to be liked? Or was it more specific than that?

Stephen said Ty liked him because he could be counted on to tell the truth without sugarcoating it and because he didn't let Ty sucker him with easy BS. Maybe Ty was drawn to Grace for similar reasons.

Ty had to prompt Sam, reminding him when it was his turn, and watched as the man halfheartedly threw. He didn't even seem to notice where his darts landed.

"I'm gonna go out on a limb here," Ty said, breaking the silence. "Woman troubles?"

After a moment's pause, Sam nodded curtly.

"Know the feeling." Ty tossed his own dart and missed by a mile. "Good luck." *We're gonna need it, brother.*

So far, both of the cooking challenges had been presented to the chefs in pristine kitchens of award-winning local restaurants—environments where Ty felt the most at home. This morning, however, Damien had summoned them to the parking lot of a gas station. Ty didn't know why they were here, but he had a bad feeling about it.

Get a grip, Beckett. If you're feeling bad, it's only because you got no sleep last night and drank enough coffee this morning to make an elephant jittery. Plus, the damp March weather would lower anyone's spirits; the sky overhead was an unforgiving gray. While not enough water was falling to qualify as actual rain, the persistent drizzle was cold. But dreary weather was no reason to psych himself out, not when each day brought him closer to his goal.

Three competitors had already been ejected from the original group. Two more would be eliminated before the festival began on St. Patrick's Day. *You can do this.* All he had to do was be the best.

After the production crew finished a quick sound-check, Damien gathered the chefs into a semicircle. Ty ended up almost directly across from Grace. His gaze lit on her, but she kept her attention fixed on the host. Was her dislike of Ty so thorough that she refused to even look in his direction?

"Good morning, chefs!" Damien began. "Some of you may be wondering why we're standing outside a convenience store. For your first two challenges, you were given access to some of the best food and beverage items the Hill Country has to offer—fresh produce, Angus beef, award-winning wines and liquor. It could be argued that even mediocre chefs can make themselves look good with such superior ingredients. Perhaps the test of a great chef is to see what he, or she, can achieve with…less impressive components."

This ominous statement was met with groans and, in Reed Lockhart's case, some imaginative swearing that Ty assumed would be edited out for television. Apparently Mr. Science had quite a mouth on him.

"For this challenge," Damien continued, "you'll be making any dish of your choosing, but you will be limited to using the foods you find inside this store, as well as some spices and basic staples from our portable *Road Trip* pantry. You have fifteen minutes to plan and shop before we're transported to the restaurant where you'll be cooking and serving the judges."

Before they'd had a chance to really process the stipulations and start strategizing, Damien's assistant held up a stopwatch and announced, "Your fifteen minutes starts *now!*"

The chefs bolted toward the small store. Ty couldn't speak for anyone else, but his haste was motivated by equal parts competitive drive and desire to get out of the blasted mist that clung to his skin and clothes. Reed and Antonio bumped each other in their hurry, and Grace's shoe slid as she entered the store, causing her to stumble. Ty reached for her, but delicately built Jo Ying had already offered a hand.

Ty straightened abruptly, shoving his own hands into his pockets, trying to look nonchalant instead of like a kid who'd dived for a baseball only to have someone else get there first. He pivoted, staring at the minimart shelves. His stomach churned as his gaze swept from the top row to the bottom.

Canned meats of mottled origin. Unnaturally orange loaves of cheeselike substance. Off-brand condensed soups and pasta meals. *I am in hell.* No, worse. He was back in his childhood.

As a chef, Ty knew all adults had specific food memories that could wring an emotional response even decades later—the homemade stew someone's mother always cooked to warm her children on rare snow days or Aunt Virginia's tangy cranberry sherbet on Thanksgiving. Donna had once begged his help trying to recreate one of Stephen's cherished childhood favorites for his thirty-fifth birthday. Ty was just like everyone else. He had *very* vivid memories of the foods he'd eaten growing up, and they invoked powerful emotions. Rage. Humiliation. Denial.

Grinding his teeth, he closed his eyes against the rows of canned goods in front of him. His childhood meals, when he was lucky enough to eat, had been foods that his school cafeteria could purchase in bulk, nonperishables supplied by a local church pantry and the canned goods Beth could get with food stamps. She always went for canned over fresh meat or produce because the canned versions were easier to cook and wouldn't spoil when the electricity was shut off—a semiregular occurrence.

When Ty had first begun to achieve some success, he'd sworn he wouldn't touch this garbage again. It was the stuff Nathan Tyler Beckett had eaten, and that scrawny trailer park boy was gone. The charity Ty was even spear-heading so that other kids—

"You okay?" Grace's voice came from directly behind him, her concern grudging but unmistakable. "What's with the statue routine? You're going to run out of time. Or ingredient choices. They're not exactly stocked for full-scale shopping sprees here."

Ty blinked. How long had he been standing frozen? "I'm fine. You should go. Shop."

"Yeah, I should totally be doing that," she agreed. "What about you?"

Since telling her he was fine had done nothing to convince her, he should just grab something—anything—to demonstrate he was participating. He glanced back to the boxes and cans in front of him, each an ugly whisper that maybe he *wasn't* good enough.

Cutting his gaze toward Grace, he demanded, "Why even bother to check on me? You made it pretty clear last night you can't stand me."

She sucked in a breath. "Maybe I only bothered because I plan to annihilate you in this competition and when I do, I want it to be because I'm inarguably the better chef. Not because you had some kind of mental break in the Fredericksburg Fuel & Food."

He pulled himself together enough to offer a ghost of his usual smile. "Bring it on, sweetheart." It wasn't her words that had cut through his paralyzing fog so much as the flare of bright uncertainty in her eyes when he'd reminded her she supposedly loathed him.

Keeping his gaze on her, he pulled a cardboard box from the shelf, managing not to flinch even though the thought of cooking any of this stuff made him want to put his fist through a wall. Peeking at what he'd chosen, he discovered it was some sort of generic macaroni mix.

She retreated a step. "I'll see you in the kitchen, Beckett."

It was probably meant to be some kind of warning that she no doubt planned to kick his butt. There was no way she could know it was the rope he was grasping to keep from falling into his past. She'd given him the boost he needed to drag himself up the rest of the aisle and down the next.

Under different circumstances, he might even have grinned. Because, whether she wanted to or not, Grace cared.

WHEN SHE'D CONFRONTED TY at the convenience store and he'd told her he was fine, Grace had wondered for just a moment if she'd exaggerated the problem in her imagination. Maybe he'd been up late with Phoebe—she struggled to ignore the instant mental images—and Ty was simply tired. But, two hours later, she knew that whatever was wrong, it was a lot worse than some missed sleep.

The kitchen was strangely subdued without him making his normal jokes and habitual small talk. He wasn't one of those people who nervously babbled in pressure situations, making everyone else want to gag him and toss his body in the nearest walk-in freezer, but he could usually be counted on to lighten the mood and update everyone on how much time remained. Today, he was quiet—except for a sharp gasp and litany of muttered curses when he burned his finger.

Grace wasn't the only one who noticed the difference in his personality.

"You all right?" Katharine asked as he rummaged through the first-aid kit. "Not like you to make mistakes."

"I make an effort to screw up every once in a while," he said. "My manager's suggestion. He says it makes me less intimidating to mere mortals." It was a typical breezy Ty Beckett response, but his voice was strained. His heart wasn't in the banter.

"What's the matter?" Stuart asked from his station. He waggled his bushy red eyebrows. "Let me guess, missing Phoebe?"

Grace stiffened at the smattering of laughter and Reed Lockhart's wolf whistle.

Katharine nipped the teasing in the bud. "Are you guys professionals or juvenile delinquents? This contest might be more interesting for me if any of you actually gave me a run for my money."

With only ten minutes left, Grace began arranging her ingredients in the waiting salad bowls, tearing open little bags of nuts and dried fruit for a finishing touch. Her dish was a curried chicken salad. She wasn't the only one using canned chicken. Katharine was doing a play on peanut butter sandwiches, tweaking an African recipe for spicy-chicken-and-peanut-butter stew and serving it between slices of bread.

Not to be outdone by Katharine's exotic choices, Reed was making individual tuna pizzas for the judges with some kind of white sauce he'd created. Grace had to assume the pizzas tasted better than they sounded. Antonio was doing stir-fry; Jo was providing the only dessert in the group, a reinterpretation of s'mores. Stuart was scrambling to put together a cold vegetable salad after his first idea fell through. Ty rounded out the group with a "gourmet macaroni and cheese." If he pulled off something truly gourmet with his Fuel & Food ingredients, Grace would be duly impressed.

She suspected that, on a good day, he could do it. But nothing about his clenched jaw or jerky movements at the stove indicated this was a good day.

Damien came through the kitchen door just as the buzzer sounded. "Time's up," he chirped.

Today, instead of serving the judges in a predetermined order and being given a chance to explain their dishes ahead of time, all of the chefs would present their food together, providing a potluck lunch for a small group of people. The chance to discuss their choices would come later, when the judges asked questions and offered commentary before they decided today's winner and loser.

The chefs returned to the kitchen to wait. They finished cleaning their stations, and those who weren't too nervous to eat tried one another's creations. Katharine opened a bottle of room-temperature merlot and asked who wanted a glass. It was usually during these moments that Ty dominated the group, keeping their nerves at bay while he praised everyone's efforts—at the same time joking that his was clearly the best. Instead, he took his glass of wine to the far side of the room and sat quietly. His features were taut, his eyes stormy. Grace had never seen him like this.

It gradually dawned on her that, despite his pensive, self-contained manner, he was angry. *Really* angry. The concept of silent fuming was foreign to her. When she was mad, there were slammed doors, wild hand gesticulations and peppery Spanish phrases. Ty's discreet approach was unnerving. Was she witnessing the calm before the storm?

Katharine sidled up to her, handing Grace an unsolicited glass of wine. "You have to talk to me," the older woman whispered. "This is just creepy. It's so quiet we could hear cheese age."

Grace nodded. "Definitely a tense vibe today."

"Most of the tension's coming from him." Katharine cut her gaze in Ty's direction. "What's going on there?"

"I have no idea. He went on a date with Phoebe last night. Maybe they argued about something?"

Katharine shook her head, dismissing Grace's bad-date theory. "I know Phoebe flirted with him whenever he was in a twenty-foot radius, but there wasn't anything serious between them. Certainly nothing to warrant so much emotion. Man looks like he's gonna go nuclear any second."

In spite of Katharine's prediction, Ty hadn't yet detonated when Damien returned to call them into the judge's panel. The seven chefs filed into a private side room normally used for birthdays, wedding rehearsal dinners and other large parties. The trio of judges sat on the opposite side of a long table—a well-dressed and unarmed firing squad. In the two previous challenges, Grace could tell from her fellow chefs' expressions whether they were feeling confident or apprehensive about their performance. But today, given the groceries they'd had to work with and the almost nonexistent guidelines on what to prepare, no one seemed to know what to expect.

The judges were Stacie Savage, a columnist from a major food magazine, retired chef Klaus Bullock, who served on the board of a regional food and wine association, and a perky executive from the corporation that owned Fuel & Food. She seemed very excited about the advertising possibilities of using today's recipes throughout the Fuel & Food chain.

As the host of the show and spokesperson for the judges, Damien announced that, on the whole, the panel was impressed with what the chefs had accomplished but that "some of you took more admirable risks than others." He named Reed the winner, which stunned Grace. Those tuna pizzas must have been *way* better than they sounded. Then the judges began offering criticism and praise for individual dishes. While they weren't shy about pointing out flaws, they were pleased overall with Grace, Antonio, Katharine and Jo. But they were scornful of Stuart's and Ty's attempts.

"That vegetable salad was a train wreck." In her critique of Stuart's work, Stacie Savage lived up to her name. "It completely lacked artistry. It tasted like something I could dump straight out of a can—although I can't imagine why I *would.* It was like a desperate, last-minute side dish you'd take to a church picnic you'd forgotten about, then slip furtively onto the table when no one was looking so they wouldn't know it was yours! You were supposed to elevate what you had to work with, but your end result was oily and lacked seasoning."

After that, there wasn't much left to say about Stuart, so they moved on to Ty. The Fuel & Food executive flashed a contrite smile. "I didn't think your mac and cheese was bad, exactly, just sort of…disappointing. I've seen you on TV and was so excited to try something you'd made. Maybe my expectations were too high."

"Chef Beckett, you were a major letdown today," the retired Chef Bullock agreed. "I happen to be a fan of up-scale mac and cheese. Chefs have done miraculous things with white cheddar, apples, truffle oil. But dumping in some hot sauce and crushing potato chips on top of rubbery pasta doesn't make it upscale anything. This was an inferior dish."

"Of course it was inferior!" Ty's voice cracked through the compact space like a whip, making several people jump. "I was shackled with inferior ingredients. How— I wouldn't have served this crap to paying customers." His eyes widened, possibly in the belated realization that he'd just insulted the judge from Fuel & Food. He opened his mouth to say more but thought better of it.

With a frustrated shake of his head, he stormed out the door. Grace had already taken a few involuntary steps in that direction before she caught herself. Biting her lip, she glanced at the judges. Was it too much to hope no one had noticed her movement?

"You've got five minutes," Damien Craig informed her. "Tell him if he's not back after that, he's disqualified."

Now that she'd had a moment to think rather than acting on sheer impulse, she wasn't sure she wanted to go after him. Right now Ty seemed as unpredictably dangerous as a wounded predator. But someone needed to talk him off the ledge.

She'd been annoyed with Ty on more than one occasion because she couldn't tell how much of what he said was sincere and how much was his slick persona, making whomever he spoke with feel special because he listened and flattered and asked follow-up questions. Whatever else could be said about his actions today, at least she knew they stemmed from genuine emotion.

Grace stepped into the corridor, wondering if he'd gone back to the kitchen or left the building entirely. *That would be bad.* He'd hate himself if he got disqualified. Thankfully she spotted him in the restaurant's empty dining room. He was gripping the back of a chair and for a moment she thought he might actually throw it, but then he slumped over it, his posture one of defeat.

She approached cautiously. "Ty?"

"Last night, you told me I'm not allowed to follow you," he said without looking up at her. "So why's it okay for you to follow me?"

She gave the kind of answer she thought he'd give if the situation was reversed. "I change the rules as I go along. It's more convenient that way."

"I screwed up royally," he said.

"I noticed." She stepped closer, reflexively placing a hand on his shoulder. The Torres family had always been pretty touchy-feely, quick to exchange hugs for bad days, good news and everything in between. "Want to tell me why?"

Straightening, he met her gaze. Raw pain shimmered in his eyes. "No. I hate talking about it. I *never* talk about it. This stupid challenge… I know why you need to win this contest, Grace, and it's a good reason. But I need to win, too. Which isn't going to happen after that dumb-ass stunt I just pulled."

"What, that little hissy fit? It'll probably add *oomph* to the episode when this airs. Viewers appreciate a few dramatic moments." She pulled her hand back to her side, disappointed not to have coaxed a smile from him. "Damien said you have five minutes to pull yourself together. Otherwise, you're out."

"I'll be eliminated anyway. They were right. That macaroni sucked. The irony is, I'm probably the best-qualified person here to work with gas station ingredients."

She cocked her head to the side. "You mean because you aren't classically trained in French cooking or a molecular gastronomist?" Ty might use down-to-earth ingredients at the core of his recipes, but he always embellished them with sophisticated touches.

"I mean…I come from nothing, Grace." He tried to sound matter-of-fact, but the undercurrent of shame in his voice wrenched her heart. "My mother got knocked up when she was a teenager, I never knew my father and we lived in trailer parks best described as crappy and crappier. Gelatinous reconstituted ham and oversalted vegetables were staples of my youth."

"A youth that's behind you," she said, awed by how far he'd come. Another time, she wanted to hear how he'd made himself a rising star in the culinary world.

"*Way* behind me," he said emphatically. "I don't even go by my given name anymore. That guy's gone. At least, I thought he was. All morning I've been stuck in some déjà vu nightmare."

"You changed your name?" Even as she asked, she felt silly—it wasn't the most pertinent part of his story. But Grace had been raised to revere her heritage. She couldn't wrap her mind around someone trying to erase who they were and where they'd come from.

He shrugged. "Started using my middle name instead. You said they gave me five minutes?"

"We should head back. You're probably down to a minute."

"Then I'll make this fast." He cupped her face. "Thank you." He bent his head and brushed his lips over hers in a caress so soft that it was more appetizer than kiss. All it did was incite a craving.

Heedless of their time limit, she stretched up on tiptoe, seeking more. Their open mouths met in a deep, hungry kiss that sizzled through her blood. It was brief, but thorough. When Ty pulled away, she stood rooted to the spot, feeling as if she'd been struck by lightning.

"Híjole."

Ty led her by the hand, tugging her toward the judging room. "Is that good or bad?"

"It's sort of all-purpose," she said breathlessly.

He stopped at the door. "After you."

"Gallantry or cowardice?" she whispered as she passed him.

"Both."

But if he was nervous about all conversation stopping as every gaze suddenly locked on him, he hid it well. He looked from person to person, meeting each judge's eyes, then expanding his focus to include the other chefs. "I apologize for any delay I caused and for my earlier unprofessional behavior. I was reacting to a personal matter and not to this competition. And, if you're gracious enough to allow my continued participation, I promise it won't happen again."

The judges exchanged glances then turned to Damien, silently signaling him. The host cleared his throat. "I've known a lot of great chefs and can say that some have been quite…temperamental."

His words earned muffled laughter from several people in the room.

"Be that as it may," Damien continued, "we don't have room for any prima donna behavior on our show."

Grace's heart thudded wildly. She wouldn't have believed she could be this anxious for one of her competitors.

"So we're going to hold you to your promise," Damien said. "It better not happen again." He turned to Stuart. "I'm sorry, Chef Capriotti, but the judges agreed your vegetable salad was the losing dish today."

Relief hit Grace so hard it nearly unbalanced her. She felt her knees sag. She darted a glance toward Ty, and even though she knew his own emotions must be twenty times what she felt, he didn't react. Instead his features remained appropriately somber, a mask of regret for his earlier actions.

As the initial tidal wave of relief ebbed, reality crept in. She was thrilled that Ty hadn't been sent home—it would be unimaginably cruel for him to lose on this particular challenge—but she still intended to win. And she couldn't do that without him being eliminated along the way.

Damien thanked the judges for their time and expertise, then reminded the contestants that tomorrow, they would face their last elimination round before the festival began. "Five of you will compete in public events at Frederick-Fest, but tomorrow will be the end of the road for someone. We'll meet on Main Street for a quick tour before you hear what the challenge is." He gave them the time and location and said they were welcome to use the *Road Trip* passenger vans or, if anyone wanted to do any sightseeing first, arrange their own transportation.

Once they'd been dismissed, Ty returned to Grace's side. "After everything else, I have no right to ask a favor, but would you mind giving me a lift? If you have to be somewhere," he said, granting her an easy out, "I can ride with the other chefs, but…"

"I'm headed to the Jalapeño. It's not too far out of my way to drop you off first." She didn't know if he planned to broach the subject of their kiss, but if so, she wanted absolute privacy.

It seemed he also wanted that privacy, but for a different reason. As soon as they were both buckled into the car, he asked, "Can I tell you a secret?"

She nodded. Was there more he needed to get off his chest about his past?

"Stephen, my manager, has been trying to negotiate an agreement with a cable channel."

Since she'd been expecting something about his adolescence, it took her a second to make the shift. But then his words fell into place. "For your own cooking show?" she guessed. Being on television had never crossed her mind until this contest—even then, it was only a means to an end, hopefully allowing her to keep the restaurant—but Ty was a natural-born host. His brief outburst this afternoon notwithstanding, had there ever been a man who was more camera-friendly? And he had the capability to charm any guests on the show into giving their best performances, too.

"It's not a done deal. But it will be if I win this competition. After today—" He broke off, looking agonized. "I can't believe how close I came to blowing it."

"For what it's worth, I think any cooking network would be crazy not to sign you."

"I don't know." He flashed a self-deprecating grin. "Word might get out that I'm difficult to work with."

"I can name a dozen celebrities who've stayed employed despite rumors of their being high-maintenance. Don't count yourself out yet, Beckett."

When she stopped in front of the inn, he gripped the door handle but didn't move.

"Ty?"

He turned toward her, his expression serious. "Thank you—for the ride, for coming after me. For caring. I let myself get psyched out over my past today and almost torpedoed my future. Whatever else happens, Grace, I'm damn grateful you're part of my present."

Chapter Seven

The Jalapeño hadn't yet opened for the evening when Grace stepped through the front door. She made a bee-line for the bar, eminently thankful that her roommate was working tonight. Amy was one of the first staff to arrive because the restaurant offered an early happy hour before the dinner rush

Amy looked up from the limes she was slicing. "How'd we do today?"

"Fair." Grace boosted herself onto a bar stool. "I didn't win the challenge, but the judges had good things to say about my dish. But today was…unexpected."

"Because of the cooking, or—" Amy stopped, study-ing her. "Never mind. You have that look again. So what did he do that was unexpected?"

"I can't decide if it's a blessing to have a friend who knows me so well or a curse," Grace grumbled. "But since I desperately need to talk to someone, we'll go with bless-ing. He kissed me."

"He what?" Amy dropped her knife. "We are talking about Ty, right? Ty Beckett, your nemesis, the guy who was in here last night flaunting his leggy blonde date?"

Grace frowned. "Oh, sure, *now* you home in on his negative qualities. Before, it's always been how hot he is and what a talented chef he is."

"All that stuff's still true," Amy said. "I'm just surprised."

"Imagine how surprised I was!"

"So what did you do?"

"Kissed him back." The memory of it sent heat coursing through her. "Which was probably a bad idea. Don't you think?"

"I don't know. You look pretty flustered. That's usually a good sign," Amy said wistfully. "Did your toes curl?"

"Ames, my toes were the *last* part of my body I was paying attention to."

Amy picked up a stack of bar napkins and fanned herself. "Doesn't sound like a mistake to me."

It hadn't felt like one, either. Not while she was caught up in the moment. The problem, of course, was that moments were so…momentary. As Ty had said when he was getting out of her car, they were part of each other's immediate present. Period. She wasn't naive enough to think there would ever be anything beyond that, especially after one of them beat the other in a challenge. Even if neither won the grand prize—a horrible worst-case scenario— there would come a day when one was eliminated.

For Ty, that had almost been today. Given how scared she'd been for him during that pulse-pounding pause before Damien sent Stuart home, she was already too emotionally invested in Chef Beckett. She doubted making out with Ty would help her regain emotional perspective. Yet whenever she thought about that kiss, she definitely wanted to repeat the mistake.

"I need to make sure he doesn't kiss me again."

"I can help with that," a male voice growled.

Grace almost fell off her bar stool. "Ben! *Híjole,* you almost gave me a heart attack."

Amy nodded in cardiac commiseration. "How can a man on crutches be stealthy?"

"Years of law-enforcement training," Ben said, maneuvering toward the stool next to Grace. "But you ladies would have seen me coming if you hadn't been so intent on your lurid conversation. What's this about some yahoo making your toes curl?"

"None of your business," Grace said tartly.

"You're my little sister," he reminded her. "Dad raised Vic and me to look out for you."

"Which is sweet, but not necessary in this case. It was an isolated incident. And I'm a grown woman. Besides, you're sworn to uphold the law. You can't run around threatening to beat up any boy who kisses me." She was still bitter about a particular high school dance her sophomore year.

Ben gave her a wide-eyed look that was half indignation, half innocence and all fraud. "Who said anything about beating up anyone? How exactly would I chase him down anyway? I'm an injured man. Then again," he added thoughtfully, "I do have a job that enables me to carry a gun."

"Oh, great. He's escalated to death threats," she groused to Amy.

Her roommate giggled. "I think it's sweet."

"You're an only child. You don't understand." Grace turned, wagging a finger at her brother. "And neither would the chief of police if he overheard you."

"Don't be too sure." Ben winked at her. "Chief has a sister and three daughters."

A classic rock song interrupted conversation, and Ben pulled his phone out of his pocket. Grace glimpsed their niece and nephew on the screen, which meant it was Victor calling.

Ben hit the answer button. "Yeah?" As he listened to whatever Victor had to say, he cut his eyes toward Grace. Then he slid rather clumsily from the stool. "I remember, but I can't discuss that at the moment. Can you hold on a second? Gracie, I'm going to borrow the office, okay?"

Grace and Victor used the office interchangeably. Ben, though being part owner, had little to do with the restaurant on a professional level.

"Of course," she said, even though she was dying to know why he needed the privacy when the only people in earshot were her and Amy, who was practically family.

They watched Ben limp away with the aid of his crutches, then exchanged glances.

"That seem weird to you?" Grace asked.

"Not as weird as Tuesday. I came in just to see if checks had been cut." Amy, like the waitstaff, made most of her money through tips, but she also drew a small biweekly salary. "Victor was sitting at a table with some man in a suit and went completely bug-eyed when he saw me. He whisked the Suit into the office like I had the plague and he was afraid it might be contagious."

"Maybe it was his lawyer," Grace mused. "They might have been discussing divorce proceedings. Victor's pretty private anyway, but he's completely embarrassed by the divorce. I feel awful for him. And for Natalie…but I'm mad at her, too. I think it's required by law, since she dumped my brother. Thank goodness you moved here when you did! Nat used to be my closest friend."

"Well, what advice do you think she would give you about Ty?"

"Being that she let go of one of the finest men I know, I'm not sure I'd want relationship tips from her. The person I really want to talk to…" Grace trailed off, thinking of all the wonderful advice her mother had given her over the years. "Never mind. I should get my butt into the kitchen."

With the festival this weekend drawing closer, they were even busier than they had been the previous night. Although the day's earlier sprinkling erupted into an earthshaking storm, the rain didn't prevent a crowd. According to Angela the waitress, they gained some travelers who'd planned to make it farther into town before stopping but, in light of the weather, opted to get off the roads for a bit.

Grace worked for hours straight, on her feet with no break. But as tiring as it was to supervise what felt like hundreds of meals, she knew it wouldn't compare to the pressure of completing tomorrow's single cooking task—whatever that may be. *The last challenge left before the finals.* She was almost halfway there!

Now was not the time to lose her head—or heart—over a sexy chef with a troubled past.

"Temptation." From his spot on the sidewalk, Damien Craig drew out the word to heighten the sense of mystery. Then he took one of those pointed pauses Ty was starting to find increasingly irksome.

They were gathered in front of a well-known chocolate shop that wasn't open to the public at this hour but whose owner had agreed to a private tasting for the chefs. Several people were fidgeting, and Ty knew he wasn't the only one who wished Damien would hurry up his speech and let them move on to the fun part. Ty liked the *Road Trip* host, but he thought the man hammed it up a bit too much. *I'll be more natural when I have my show, less stilted.*

Damien lowered his voice. "What tempts you?"

At that, Ty's mental critique came to a screeching halt.

He knew all too well what—*who*—tempted him. He'd thought about her last night both in his waking thoughts and in his dreams. His gaze slid to Grace, who stood on the other side of Antonio. From Ty's vantage point, he could only see her profile, but that was more than enough to recall yesterday, his mouth on hers.

After getting so mind-whacked during that awful Fuel & Food challenge, he'd expected to once again have trouble sleeping. But he'd been out as soon as his head hit the pillow, sweetly tormented by images of Grace's body beneath his.

With a start, Ty realized he was having a highly inappropriate response in the middle of a filmed segment. He averted his gaze, mentally calculating measurement tables as he stared at the damp sidewalk. *Three teaspoons equals one tablespoon, five tablespoons plus one teaspoon equals a third of a cup...* After a few moments had passed, he was once again able to concentrate on the lecture they were receiving about the chocolate shop.

The founder had studied with a Swiss master chocolatier, learning a centuries-old European art of perfecting liquid-center chocolates, rather than simply injecting empty chocolate shells with liquid. "The result," Damien said, "is fantasy in the form of confection. You should all try the house specialty, a divine chocolate with separate and distinct layers of almond and tequila. Every bite sold in there is one of absolute decadence—liquid temptation in spun crystals and chocolate coating."

"This is so my challenge!" Pastry chef Jo Ying declared.

"I don't know about that," Katharine rejoined, "but it's sounding a lot more enjoyable than yesterday's."

"This field trip is meant to inspire you," Damien told them. "While you aren't required to use chocolate, you should come up with the most tempting dessert you can think of—sinful luxury on a plate. You're also tasked with naming the dish and telling the judges why they should be tempted to make you the winner. Remember, this is your last chance to get into the finals. Make it count."

Finally he grinned. "Who's ready for some chocolate?"

They entered the store with a great deal of enthusiasm. Jo immediately struck up conversation with a woman behind the counter, asking her about the finer points of their technique. Ty nodded absently at an observation Reed made about the density of sugar crystals, then headed for Grace. She stood in front of a case of coffee-based chocolates.

He nodded toward the espresso-filled. "That's one way to get your morning caffeine."

"Speaking from past experience, they're addictive. Probably a billion calories, but completely worth it. This is my favorite challenge by far." Grace wrinkled her nose. "Although you realize, by afternoon, we'll all have lapsed into sugar comas."

He laughed. "Not if we use a bit of self-control." *Hypocrite.* Where was his self-control when he'd kissed her mere yards from the judging table? "You just have to know when to stop."

She gave him a sidelong look. "So you don't have any trouble with willpower? Amy and I discussed this at the restaurant last night. There's a big difference between knowing you shouldn't have something and wanting it anyway."

"True." His body moved toward her of its own volition, not quite pressing her into the glass case but certainly closer than he had any business being. "Maybe the trick is to indulge only a little. A taste couldn't hurt, right? Just enough to satisfy the craving."

Grace's eyes were wide, luminous pools. Her breathing grew choppy.

"Good morning!" A cheerful woman in a monogrammed apron leaned on the counter. "Have you two decided what you want?"

Stammering as if they'd been caught naked by a nun, Grace whirled away from him. "N-no! I...I mean— Ty? Do you?"

"Know what I want?" He smiled lazily. "I have a few ideas."

Grace glared. "I'll bet."

Lord, she was adorable. And sexy as hell. He hadn't known many women who could be both at the same time. "Tell me what's good, Grace," he suggested. "I'm open to direction."

Her eyes narrowed. "Knock it off, Beckett."

"What?" he asked innocently. "You're the local who's been here before. I value your palate."

He watched her wrestle with a smile and lose. It broke across her face like dawn.

"You're incorrigible," she said, laughter in her eyes.
And you're beautiful.

The forgotten employee heaved a sigh. "So have either of you made a selection? There are other people I could help."

"Sorry, ma'am." Ty tried to mollify her with a remorseful tone and a practiced sheepish smile. "It's just that everything looks so good it's impossible to choose. What's *your* favorite?"

She brightened once more. "Oh, that would have to be in our line of fruit centers."

As she burbled on happily about the black-cherry filling, Ty saw Grace roll her eyes in his peripheral vision, wordlessly heckling him. Like his manager, Grace definitely saw through his charm. But after the way she'd kissed him back yesterday and the telltale signs of arousal this morning, he no longer believed she was immune to him. *No more than I am to her.*

He didn't have the first clue what he was going to make for this challenge, but he was supposed to name it something that encompassed temptation. At the moment, he couldn't think of anything in the world more tempting than Grace.

FOR GRACE, FOOD HAD ALWAYS been a sensory experience—she loved the textures and aromas and colors almost as much the flavors—but this was the first time it had felt like such an unbearably sensual experience. Everywhere she turned, there was the slow drizzle of chocolate or the sticky sweetness of honey or the silky cling of powdered sugar. She didn't know if she had the best recipe in the kitchen, but she was cooking with plenty of passion. Shouldn't that earn her some points?

After yesterday's fiasco, Ty had reverted to his normal self. He was mock-swooning over how good Katharine's dessert smelled while good-naturedly taunting Reed and Antonio. It seemed he had a smile and a jest for everyone—except Grace. When he looked at her, the humor in his blue-gray eyes was replaced by something far more intense, nearly predatory. She shivered, unable to look away as he came closer.

"Cream-filled beignets?" The hunger in his expression belied his casual tone.

She nodded. "I'm calling them 'Simple Seduction.' They may not be the fanciest dish presented today, but there's a lot to be said for a classic. Besides, they remind me…" Her cheeks warmed. "I went to New Orleans with some friends once. Turned out to be a very, um, enjoyable trip."

Ty groaned. "You're killing me," he said under his breath. "You'd better practice what you say to the judges, Grace. I swear I can see everything you're remembering on your face."

She believed him. But her embarrassment was minor compared to the wicked urge to tease him. "*Every*thing? Goodness. Should I get you some ice?" she asked. "I'd hate for you to overheat."

He leaned so close she couldn't help scanning the kitchen to see if anyone was watching. His breath brushed her ear. "I survived kissing you, sweetheart, and it doesn't get much hotter than that."

While she was scrambling for a reply, he grinned and returned to his station. She was so relieved when their time was up, she almost forgot to be nervous about the judging. It looked like stiff competition today. Damien told them that the judges really had to work to come up with their decision. But Antonio's rum cake "Yo ho!" with its bananas, chocolate chips, dark rum and ganache was ultimately ruled the loser.

As a baker from San Marcos put it, "From the name to the decorating, the cake was really more playful than decadent. And with all the different ingredients, it had an 'everything but the kitchen sink' feel."

One of the other guest judges hastened to add, "It was still a great slice of cake. In another challenge, against other entries, it might have won."

Grace was a mass of conflicting emotions as she hugged the burly man goodbye. Antonio had been a friend of her dad's and always kind to her. She genuinely liked him, but, with a chef of his experience gone, had her chances improved?

She was thrilled the judges enjoyed her dish—and that she got through her edited explanation of why she'd chosen beignets without stuttering. They also raved about Katharine's cheesecake and Reed's citrus crème brûlée. When Grace had heard that Ty's dish—a dark-chocolate cake topped with chipotle caramel sauce—was called "Kissed By Fire," her pulse had accelerated rapidly, thudding in her ears. She felt as if he'd just announced on national television that they'd kissed. *Once. You're both experienced adults. It shouldn't be that big of a deal.*

But it undeniably was.

To no one's surprise, Jo won the challenge with her apple tart in a chocolate walnut crust, which she'd called "Worth the Fall." She'd joked while they waited during deliberation that it was a shame none of the judges were named Eve.

When they were dismissed for the day, Grace escaped to her car without sticking around to say farewell or congratulations to the other finalists. Even though she told herself her hurry was to see her mother, she knew perfectly well that she was avoiding Ty. *Temptation, indeed.* She'd concluded logically that they shouldn't have kissed and certainly shouldn't do anything more. Yet the way he'd looked at her all day…

She thought wryly of Jo's dessert. There might not have been an Adam or Eve around, but that didn't mean no one had fallen.

"Do you need some help?" The woman at the front desk eyed Grace's struggles with amusement.

"I think I've got it now. But thanks." Grace carried a cardboard box of decorations, but as she'd come through the entryway of Gunther Gardens, the bottom of the container had given out. It had taken some quick juggling to keep everything from falling. Thank goodness there was nothing heavy in the assortment. She settled her unwieldy armful on the counter while she signed the visitor log.

The receptionist pushed her glasses farther up on her nose. "You're here for Mrs. Torres in 18, right?"

Grace nodded. "Mom always got a big kick out of St. Patrick's Day, so I brought her some gold and green to spruce up her room."

"Someone else had the same thought. I believe she's still with your mom now." The woman flipped back a page and tapped a line of the register. "Yep. Hasn't signed out yet."

Grace recognized the familiar signature even before her mind processed the letters she was reading: Natalie Torres. It suddenly occurred to Grace that although she'd warned Victor about Colleen's fanciful musing that Natalie was pregnant, she really should have alerted her sister-in-law, as well. It wasn't fair to let Natalie walk into such a potentially awkward conversation uninformed. *I'm glad she's here.* Grace had avoided her for too long already.

As she made her way down the hall, Grace recalled one of her classmates in middle school telling her how lucky she was. "Your family has a party for *everything,*" the girl had said enviously. "My parents' idea of celebrating is ordering a pizza on my birthday and showering me with gift certificates—not that I'm complaining about the gift certificates." It was true the Torres household had been a lively one. There was a big bash for every birthday, a neighborhood cookout for Cinco De Mayo and a gathering for St. Patrick's Day. Grace remembered how her mom would stage elaborate "leprechaun pranks" that usually made Grace and her brothers laugh themselves silly. And during Grace's elementary school years, Colleen organized a St. Patrick's Day search in the backyard for gold coins, really foil-wrapped chocolates. The little boy who lived next door to them once demanded to know why she got two Easter egg hunts each year.

Now that Grace stopped to think about it, she realized this was the first year in memory that they weren't doing something special at the restaurant in observation of St. Patrick's Day. She'd been too wrapped up with the competition to think about it. Besides, after tonight, she didn't expect much business for the rest of the weekend. While Frederick-Fest occurred every March, it was just serendipity that it began on St. Patrick's Day this year. Hundreds of tourists and most of the town would be attending. While she hadn't officially closed the Jalapeño for Saturday and Sunday, she'd only scheduled a skeleton crew. Amy and Ben, Angela and Rosie and two of the restaurant's line cooks would work in pairs at the festival, taking turns manning a booth on Main Street where they offered free samples and other promotional goodies to the crowd.

She'd been a little surprised when Ben volunteered so eagerly, but as he put it, "If my leg were healed, I'd be on crowd-control detail. Since I can't do that, at least this gives me a chance to be useful."

Participating in the festival was probably of greater marketing value than hosting a St. Patrick's party at the restaurant, but still, she felt a little melancholy to think she'd inadvertently dropped one of her mom's traditions. *Next year we'll do something big.* Assuming, of course, that the restaurant was still open this time next year.

Taking a deep breath and balancing her box against one hip, she knocked at her mom's door. Today, it wasn't Colleen who answered but *Tía* Maria.

"Graciela!" For such a deceptively frail-looking woman, Grace's aunt was certainly capable of bone-crushing hugs.

The box of decorations tumbled to the floor. "It's a regular fiesta in here now. Colleen, I'm going to start spending all my evenings in your apartment. I didn't realize it was such a popular destination."

Colleen stepped forward to hug her daughter, but her gaze wasn't as sharp as it had been last time Grace visited. Her expression was vaguely troubled, as if she was uncertain why her tiny apartment was suddenly full of people.

When Grace looked over her mom's shoulder, she spotted Natalie standing by the couch, shifting her weight from one foot to the other. Natalie was tall for a woman and had always towered over Grace, but something about the look on her face made her seem a lot smaller today.

Natalie cleared her throat, fiddling with one of the light brown corkscrew curls that framed her face. "Hi, Grace. I was about to leave, so don't worry about me being in the way."

Leaving because she no longer felt welcome, or because she was ducking Grace just as Grace had been dodging her? "Wait, Nat. I…" Casting a glance at her mom, Grace rethought her words. She'd been about to invite Natalie to stay, but Colleen really was looking overwhelmed. So instead, she asked, "How about I walk you out and we detour through the cafeteria? They have pretty good coffee and all-day bakery selections."

Not that Grace planned to order anything sweet. It would be days before she could look at a dessert without thinking of Ty and feeling feverish. She shifted her attention to Maria. "If that's all right with you? I'll be back in a few minutes."

Maria nodded, patting Colleen on the hand. "I'll stay with her until you get back. You two should chat." Maria had always doted on Victor, and her voice lost some of its warmth when she addressed his soon-to-be-ex-wife. "It was thoughtful of you to bring by the window ornament."

Grace followed her aunt's gaze to the window behind the sofa. They'd hung a painted glass leprechaun dancing beneath a brilliant rainbow. The afternoon sunlight sparkling through the decoration made it the brightest thing in the room.

"That's lovely," Grace said.

Natalie shrugged uncomfortably. "She's always loved St. Pat's. And I've always loved her," she added, her eyes watery.

Uh-oh. Grace decided they should definitely excuse themselves before this conversation got any more emotional. Maria had led Colleen to her favorite chair, and Grace knelt at her mother's side. "I'll be right back, okay?"

"All right." But Colleen was peering past her, eyes unfocused.

Grace bit her lip. Victor had tentatively planned to take their mom to the festival tomorrow, just as she'd taken them for years. She loved the event. But Grace wondered if the crowds and constant sensory stimulations would be too much. The noise and sheer number of people were enough to give anyone a moment's disorientation.

As she got to her feet, Grace asked Natalie, "You good with the coffee plan?"

Her sister-in-law nodded. "Yeah, but it'll have to be decaf for me. I'm already too on edge these days."

The two women walked wordlessly to the cafeteria, where they ordered and paid for their respective beverages. Grace got the impression they both wanted to clear the air but that neither knew how to begin. As they sat at a corner table on the far side of the room, she blurted the unvarnished truth.

"You look as bad as he does." If they were so miserable apart, why couldn't they have made things work together?

Natalie sniffed. "Thanks. I figured I probably looked way worse than him. You know how collected Vic is in a crisis. I, on the other hand, am a mess." Her eyes welled with tears. "The kids are furious with me. Everyone in town thinks of me as Mrs. Victor Torres and probably always will. Hell, I still think of myself that way. And you probably hate me."

"I don't hate you." Grace sighed. "I just feel sick for both of you. I don't... You told him he was sucking the joy out of your life?"

"Not one of my finer moments." Natalie dumped three packets of sugar into her coffee. "I was frustrated, and he was being deliberately obtuse. Victor's a highly intelligent man and when I tried to tell him how I felt, I got the feeling he didn't want to understand."

"Well, try explaining it to me. Let's see if I can get it."

Natalie dragged the stirring stick listlessly through her drink, then added another sugar for good measure. "Did you notice a change in him after your dad died?"

"I'm not sure," Grace admitted. "We were all devastated. Honestly I was too wrapped up in my own grief and Mom's to be well attuned to anyone else."

"Vic shut me out. I thought maybe it was a guy thing, that he didn't know how to let himself be vulnerable. But it got worse." Nervously Natalie pulled another packet from the sugar holder.

Five? But Grace held her tongue. If they had to sacrifice an innocent cup of coffee to repair their friendship, it was worth it.

"I don't know if Victor tells you much about his job. He stopped confiding in me about a year ago, but he's had some grim moments. Customers defaulting on loans, people losing their houses, businesses going under. Between that and your dad and then your mom's declining health… All of a sudden, he could only see the negative in the world. Like if he woke up with so much as a stomachache, he'd immediately remind me where the life insurance paper was in case he dropped over dead before lunch."

Grace fought the traitorous compulsion to snicker. Of the three Torres siblings, Victor had always been the most naturally cautious, which had led to some funny childhood anecdotes, such as the time he'd tried to bubble wrap his room after breaking a toe. That very vigilance was why she'd assumed his marriage would be rock solid— because he'd been so careful to only ask someone he felt one hundred percent sure of and because he'd seemed like the type of husband who would do damage control before any problem grew out of hand.

"You're exaggerating," she chided Natalie.

"I am, and I'm not. He became so fixated on preparing himself for worst-case scenarios that he didn't realize he was creating one. Any time I tried to do something fun for us, for the kids, he made me feel it was trivial. The way he talked about off-loading the restaurant that was practically his second home because he was afraid, saying it would drag everyone into debt? He was teaching our kids not to dream, to cower rather than reach for their goals."

That stung. Grace was all too aware that he thought the logical thing to do was sell The Twisted Jalapeño.

When Natalie reached for another packet of sugar, Grace grimaced. "Uh…you're not planning to drink that, are you?"

"Lord, no. I just need something to play with. I've been so jittery lately. I've started to sympathize with why people smoke." She exhaled, crumpling the empty sugar packet with the others. "I saw him changing right in front of me, but I didn't handle it well. At first, I was too subtle, trying to get him to notice the problem without directly confronting him. As my irritation grew, I retaliated with snarky comments that didn't help either of us. When I got desperate enough to acknowledge how far apart we'd drifted, I made a concerted effort. You babysat the kids for us one night, and I took him out to dinner."

"I remember. I was stunned when the two of you split up so soon after your romantic evening."

"Romantic? Hardly. He took the stance that since he still told me he loved me every day and still kissed me goodbye each morning, he couldn't possibly be withdrawn. We fought, and he slept on the couch. He seemed to believe I was inventing problems that didn't exist because I *wanted* out. When I mentioned counseling, he was apathetic. It was that doomsday attitude again—like we were over, so what was the point of fighting the inevitable? Can I tell you something awful?"

"It gets worse?" She prayed Natalie wouldn't say she'd been unfaithful. It would be difficult to forgive that kind of betrayal to her brother.

"When I asked for the divorce, I think, subconsciously, that I did it to shock him. I was hoping he'd snap out of it. But he called my bluff, didn't he? Calmly packed his suitcase and relocated to Ben's." The tears that had been threatening all afternoon spilled forth. "Now he's taking the next step and getting his own place, which means he's…he's r-really not coming back. Ever."

This was the first Grace had heard of him moving. He hadn't even said anything to her about looking. "How do you know he's getting a place?"

"The meetings he's had with agents," Natalie sobbed.

"One of the other PTA moms is a receptionist for a real-estate office."

The Suit. Grace jerked upright in her chair. The pieces fit—that meeting Amy had accidentally interrupted, the one Vic so adamantly hadn't wanted her to overhear. And the morning earlier this week when he'd once again tried to convince Grace to give up the "stress" of their family legacy. Not to mention his call to Ben yesterday, the one that had made her brother eye her guiltily and scuttle off like a cockroach seeking shelter. So incensed she could barely see straight, Grace let loose a stream of blistering Spanish.

When the worst of it had run its course, she said in English, "I don't think Victor's looking for a permanent place to live. He's looking for a buyer. Those bastards are planning to sell my restaurant out from under me!"

Chapter Eight

Seemingly all of Fredericksburg and most of the surrounding counties were headed downtown for the morning parade that officially kicked off Frederick-Fest. But Ty
and the other three finalists who'd been staying at the inn
were going against traffic, en route to another restaurant
kitchen. Once they arrived, he found himself automatically scanning the premises—not for a clue about today's
challenge, but for any sign of Grace.

She'd left yesterday without saying goodbye, which had
chafed more than he would have imagined. He and the
other chefs at the hotel had taken Antonio out for dinner
last night to send him off in style; though Ty had enjoyed
himself, he wished Grace could have joined them. Antonio himself had called her at the Jalapeño, but since it
had been a Friday night and the town was bursting at the
seams with visitors, no one had been surprised that she
had to work.

Damien was still consulting with the production crew
when the kitchen door swung open and Grace walked in.

"Whoa," Reed said under his breath. He poked Ty in
the shoulder. "Is there a Cordon Bleu school for ninjas I
don't know about?"

She looked in the mood to kick some serious ass. Her
chef jacket was draped over her arm. She wore a black

tank top with fitted black pants far more sinful than any of yesterday's supposedly decadent desserts. Her hair, which was normally loosely pulled back when she cooked, had been ruthlessly tamed into a tight, high ponytail that reminded Ty of femme fatales from sixties' spy movies—the kind who could kill a man over martinis as easily as seduce him. Her only flash of color came from a pair of sparkling green stud earrings he assumed were a nod to the holiday.

The overall effect was lethally sexy, with only one flaw.

If a person looked closely—and Ty had fallen into the habit of watching her *very* closely—he could detect something haunted in her eyes that didn't match the rest of her take-no-prisoners look. The bleakness in her expression was subtle, but it was there. He wanted to hold her, ask her what was wrong and how he could help, but he knew she wouldn't welcome such unprofessional behavior in this setting. And her demeanor suggested today was the wrong time to cross her.

Instead of giving in to the impulse to go to her, he remained where he was, offering a friendly wave while she shrugged into her jacket. She tipped her head in acknowledgment, but didn't smile or wave back. The teasing playfulness that had brightened her gaze yesterday had been extinguished.

When it was time to begin, Damien reminded them that from now on, they wouldn't only be serving the judges. Their food would also be available to members of the general public, who would be allowed to vote on their top choices.

"Your dishes today and tomorrow will be presented anonymously to minimize any advantage that, say, a local favorite might have." At this, he guffawed in Grace's direction as if he'd made a particularly clever joke.

She eyed the host with an unblinking stare that made Ty want to hide all the sharp objects in the kitchen. Damien should probably refrain from chortling in her direction.

"Since today is St. Patrick's Day," the man continued, "it seemed fitting we do an Irish-themed challenge. Your task today is to make your own adaptation of a dish generally associated with Ireland."

Ty couldn't help recalling poor Seamus Wilson, who'd been sent home on the first challenge. The Irishman would have had a natural advantage.

Grace's mother was also Irish. He dared another look in her direction. Did her dark mood have anything to do with her mom? Worry clouded his thoughts, obliterating any creative brilliance on what recipe he should tackle.

Damien herded them toward the vans, where they'd have their only chance to brainstorm before shopping for ingredients. "This afternoon, you'll be transporting your dishes to the *Road Trip* pavilion at the festival, where they'll be displayed with a number for voting purposes. And the big news is…no one will be eliminated today! Your scores will be combined with tomorrow's scores and the person whose cumulative work is judged the lowest will be out. So everyone will have this evening to enjoy the festival."

Ha. They'd all have the evening to stress over how they'd done and speculate fruitlessly on the judges' opinions as they rolled into tomorrow's event.

Since the chefs fell into a group as they exited the building, it was easier to approach Grace without being obvious. "Happy St. Pat's," he said lightly.

She kept her gaze straight ahead, her body rigid. "Back at you."

He frowned. What had happened to the temptress who had laughingly offered to bring him ice because it was getting so hot in the kitchen? "Grace." He cupped her shoulder to slow her down, lowering his voice. "You were there for me the other day. If there's any way I can return the favor…"

She smiled tremulously. "I appreciate that, Ty. Really."

But when she gently pulled away and angled toward a different van than the one he boarded, he was no closer to understanding what had gone wrong.

CHOPPING VEGETABLES, GRACE reflected, was a lot easier when a person's hands weren't shaking. Ever since her revelation yesterday afternoon, she'd been literally vibrating with anger. Naturally last night had been one of the few when neither of her skunk brothers showed up at the restaurant. Coincidence, or were they already meeting with prospective buyers behind her back? On one hand, she was grateful not to have encountered either of them. She needed to focus her energy on winning this, and she suspected the coming confrontation would be draining. Plus, it was bad form for a chef to threaten to disembowel her siblings with an entire dining room of customers in earshot.

On the other hand, her rage was festering in an unhealthy way. The anger roiling in her was so potent it was difficult to think about anything beyond their betrayal. *They promised, dammit!* If she won, she got to keep the restaurant. That was the deal. The harsh reality was that her brothers could outvote her and sell, but she'd never dreamed they'd instigate the process without involving her at all. Had Victor given up trying to talk sense into her and simply gone around her? For weeks, she'd felt torn between her loyalty to him as family and to Natalie as a friend, but at the moment, she found herself falling firmly in Natalie's camp.

"Careful, there," Ty advised on a trip back from the pantry. "You're whacking those veggies with a lot of… verve. Why not take a short break? Get a glass of water, count your fingers. Make sure there are still ten."

She felt the corner of her mouth twitch. It said a lot about Ty's appeal that he could wring even a partial smile from her in her current mood. "If I do cut myself, at least you can show me where the first-aid kit is," she said, referencing his burn earlier this week.

"That's one option." His lips curved into that grin that made her knees go liquid. "For any minor scrape or contusion, I'd also be willing to kiss it better."

"Such a giver," she murmured.

Their eyes locked. It wasn't until she looked away that she realized it was the first minute she'd spent all day when her brother's perfidy hadn't been foremost in her mind. Her gratitude was tempered with sudden shyness. What did it say about her that a man she'd known a week had temporarily blotted out her family and the restaurant that meant the world to her?

She swallowed. "So…what are you cooking? If you don't mind my asking."

He tilted his head, regarding her seriously. "Ask me anything you want, Grace."

What's your first name? She hadn't realized she was curious until the question popped into her head. She wouldn't ask, of course. It was inconsequential and invasive. He'd made it clear how hard he'd worked to distance himself from who he'd once been.

"Corned beef and cabbage," he said. "My twist is that I'm grilling it."

She rolled her eyes. "Of course you are."

"Don't knock it till you've tried it, sweetheart." He hesitated. "You know, before I leave Fredericksburg, I want to cook for you. If you'll let me."

Cook for her as in a *date?* "I…" She clutched her knife like a security blanket. "I have a lot of chopping to finish."

"I'll get out of your way." His eyes twinkled mischievously. "But you know where I am if you acquire any boo-boos."

WHEN DAMIEN ANNOUNCED that it was time to pack up their food for transport to the festival, Grace tried to assess how her dish would measure up against the others. She had to admit Katharine's lamb stew smelled amazing, and she assumed Jo had done a competent job with her Irish soda bread—although it might be too simplistic an offering compared to the others. Reed Lockhart was clearly insane. Citing the importance of potatoes in Irish history, Mr. Science had used his distinctive background in molecular gastronomy to make a potato foam gnocchi. Grace was pretty sure the only foam the crowd wanted on St. Patrick's Day was topping their beer, but she kept that opinion to herself.

She was fairly proud of her shepherd's pie, which was shaped more like pizza pie. In a slight reverse on the usual dish, she'd used mashed potatoes to make a crust of sorts, then filled it in with savory fresh vegetables and beef she'd soaked in a Guinness marinade.

Finally there was Ty and his corned beef. Her mind tried to veer away from the look he'd given her earlier, half invitation and half dare, but she could no longer compartmentalize him as merely a fellow contestant. How had he become so much more to her in such a short time?

She was unsurprised when he slid onto the bench seat next to her. Jo sat in front of them, but with the radio playing and the pastry chef leaning forward to converse with the production assistant who was driving, it felt as if Ty and Grace were in their own little bubble. He was so close and her heart was so heavy, it was tempting to rest her head on his shoulder. He wouldn't mind.

If there's any way I can return the favor, he'd said. She'd had to end her visit with Natalie yesterday because she'd wanted to have plenty of time with her mom. Since sharing her accusation with Nat, she hadn't discussed it with anyone else. Could she vent to Ty about something so personal?

Not about the restaurant, not with its future on the line. He'd told her the other day that he understood why she needed to win, but that he had his own motivations driving him. God, when she thought of what he'd endured as a kid—a life she couldn't even fathom—she lost any urge to whine to him. She hated the thought that she'd sound self-pitying.

Also, while it could be confusing at times, she was enjoying the flirtatious truce between them. They were relating to each other as friends, possibly more, and if she started blithering about how much she needed this win, it would be an awkward reminder that only one of them could come out on top.

Oblivious to her internal struggle—or simply respectful of her privacy—Ty stared out the window instead of quizzing her on what was wrong. He seemed dazed by the sheer number of people on the streets and sidewalks. "Wow, I thought some of the talk I'd heard was exaggeration, but you guys really draw a crowd."

"The festival attracts vendors from all over the country," she said proudly. "Word has spread, and lots of people want in on the action. Of course, the majority are still from Texas. We prefer it that way."

He swiveled his head back toward her. "The other day, I mentioned how I wanted to get as far from my upbringing as possible?"

She nodded tentatively, surprised he'd broached the subject.

"The most obvious solution, after I'd finally earned a little money, was to start fresh somewhere and leave Texas. But I just couldn't. Don't know why, it's not like I'm tethered by happy childhood memories. I guess this place is in my blood."

"Because you're a true Texan," she said. "You're everything we're known for—bold, resourceful, engaging. Stubborn as hell," she added impishly.

"That's listed as 'persistent' on my résumé."

"Well, I for one am glad you're here and not on some far-flung coast."

His hand slid discreetly over hers, and he squeezed her fingers. "Me, too."

Secretly holding hands with a guy in the back of a van made her feel fifteen again, with that same giddy rush that accompanies young love. Only now, instead of the vague anxiety over what she should do if the object of her affection returned her interest, the adrenaline and wicked thrill were coupled with the desires of a grown woman.

"Grace." His low tone was nearly hypnotic. "Once we're done at the pavilion, will you spend the rest of the afternoon with me? Show me the festival? I'd like to see it through your eyes."

How could she possibly turn down a request like that? "All right." When her voice came out huskier than normal, she blushed and tried to adjust her tone to breezy nonchalance. "Just picture me as your tour guide."

He didn't answer, but his gaze swept over her slowly before returning to meet hers. He raised an eyebrow.

"Suddenly I'm worried we have two very different ideas of what a tour guide should look like," she said, wishing the driver would crank up the air-conditioning. It might only be March on the calendar, but that was still Texas sun streaming through the windows.

Ty grinned unrepentantly. "My imagination, my rules."

Oh, my. A braver woman might ask just exactly what was running through his imagination. Instead she gave him an inscrutable Mona Lisa smile and let him wonder what was going on in *hers.*

As she stepped down from the van, she realized one of the things she needed to do this afternoon wouldn't be particularly festive. "After we get our food set up, I have to take care of an…errand. I'll understand if you don't want to wait for me. We can meet later."

"Trying to get rid of me already?" He said it lightly. Was she imagining the slim thread of vulnerability in his voice?

"You can come with me," she relented. He wouldn't understand most of the exchange, anyway.

IT WOULD BE A WASTE OF Grace's time to try tracking down Victor in this throng. Besides, she couldn't give him a piece of her mind if he was with their mom. She wouldn't run the risk of upsetting Colleen.

Ben, however, was fair game.

And she knew just where to find him. "I need to stop by our booth. The Twisted Jalapeño's," she clarified. "Amy and my brother should be there."

"Which brother is that?" Ty asked.

"The cop." Who saw it as his duty to serve and protect total strangers but had no compunction about lying to his only sister.

Ty was quiet, but she could feel him studying her as she dashed through the crowd. She wanted to pin down Ben before shifts changed at the booth.

"So, who's responsible for the smoke coming out of your ears?" Ty ventured. "Amy, or the brother?"

She didn't bother denying her anger. "The brother. Both brothers, actually, but one can deliver a message to the other. If I let him live." She snapped her fingers. "There they are!"

Not bothering to wait for Ty—she knew he'd catch up—she barreled toward the booth. If she'd been in a more rational frame of mind, she might have taken a moment to examine how closely Ben and Amy sat, the way they were looking at each other. But now was not the time to speculate on her brother's romantic interests. It was his property dealings that concerned her.

"Ben!"

"Hey, sis." He did a double take, getting a better look at her expression. "Something wrong?"

"You tell me." Her gaze flickered in Amy's direction, a cursory greeting before she zeroed in on her brother. "That phone call the other day? When Victor called you at the restaurant and you slunk away like a thief in the night?"

Ben had gone pale beneath his naturally swarthy skin tone. "Now, Grace, you have to understand. Victor just wants—"

"Don't you *dare* defend him!" The guilt in her brother's eyes was like a dagger. On some level, she'd been hoping he'd ask what the heck she was talking about. In this case, she would have been happy to have been wrong.

Amy glanced wide-eyed between the two of them. "Someone want to tell me what's going on?"

"I'll fill you in at home," Grace said. "Right now, I can't even find the words. I'm so mad I could…" Despite what she'd just said, plenty of words burbled up inside her. She let loose a cannon volley of heated Spanish slang.

"You know," a voice commented behind her, "I'm beginning to understand how Lucy felt."

Confusion temporarily penetrated her hurt. "Lucy who?" she asked Ty.

"Ricardo. As in *I Love Lucy*. Classic. Surely you've seen an episode or two? Her husband launched into these Spanish tirades she couldn't translate." He disarmed her with a grin, then peered around her to nod at the two in the booth. "Amy, nice to see you again. I didn't catch your name, though."

"Officer Ben Torres."

"Ty Beckett. Can I give you a friendly piece of advice, Officer? Don't tick off your sister. She's scary dangerous. Now please tell her you're sorry for whatever you screwed up because she promised to show me around."

Grace shot her brother a warning glance. No way was a rote "I'm sorry" going to end this. There was plenty to be discussed. But Ty had managed to defuse the worst of her immediate anger. Sampling local cuisine and indulging in the nostalgia of kitschy carnival rides sounded far more pleasurable than listening to her brother make excuses.

"We'll talk later," she told Ben sweetly, taking vindictive glee in the beads of sweat that had appeared on his forehead. "Amy, I'll see you tonight."

"Or not." Her roommate gave Ty an approving nod. "I won't wait up."

Grace's cheeks heated. She waited until she and Ty

had moved away from the table before remarking, "Don't mind Amy. She's—"

"I like her," he interrupted. "Jury's still out on your brother, though. What did he do to set you off like that?"

She sighed. Since she'd aired her dirty laundry in front of him, she might as well give him the reason. "The Twisted Jalapeño needs work. Some remodeling, some marketing, some improvements to the parking lot. But we were determined to get Mom the best care possible, which, as you can imagine, isn't cheap. The truth is, the restaurant hasn't been the same since Dad died. I want to revitalize it, but Victor's leery of sinking more money into it. Neither of my brothers has any interest in running it. The perfect solution would be for me to buy them out, but I don't have that kind of capital."

Not without the contest prize money. Even then, she'd need to secure a loan for repairs. But she was hoping the publicity of a win would bring in enough customers to help pay off bills.

"My brothers and I had a deal," she said haltingly. "At least I thought we did. If I don't win *Road Trip,* I let them sell."

"Grace." Ty stopped, his expression stricken.

She bulldozed over him, unable to dwell on how much they each needed to win. "I thought I had a stay of execution, time to get the word out about me and the restaurant. But now I learn my brothers are meeting with real-estate agents. I don't know whether they're planning to sell either way or if they just don't have faith that I can win. I'm surprised there's not a big For Sale sign slapped on the front of the building." She gave a fierce shake of her head. "I'm being lousy company. We're supposed to be having fun."

"I shouldn't have imposed myself on you," he said, his words barely audible.

"You're not an imposition. You're a welcome distraction from my sudden homicidal desire to be an only child. Come on, it's St. Patrick's Day! We need to find a couple of beers and get in the festival spirit."

He held her gaze a long time before nodding. "All right."

As they passed a table selling cheerfully tacky accessories—headbands sporting shamrock antennae, battery-operated necklaces strung with flashing emerald beads—she had a sudden realization. "You're not wearing anything green!"

"Do you know that for a fact?" he challenged with a gleam in his eye.

She took in his jeans and the Dallas Cowboys shirt he'd worn beneath his chef's jacket. The dark blue T-shirt brought out his eyes, but she didn't see green anywhere. Was he wearing it beneath those attractively snug jeans? Heat suffused her as she imagined scenarios in which she could find out.

"Ms. Torres, I'm shocked at you," he fibbed. They both knew he was too shameless to shock. "For your information, I'm wearing green socks."

She punched him in the shoulder. "You're terrible."

"Me? You were the one with your mind in the gutter. Don't deny it."

She conveniently changed the subject. "Where to first? There are performances, craft booths, midway rides, rodeo demonstrations and enough concessions to keep us stuffed into next month."

"Lady's choice. What's your favorite thing to do here?"

"I love it all," she admitted. "The people-watching, the

tamales, the souvenir beer steins, the rickety rides that spin me until I feel sick, the smell of hay at the livestock barn, the way my fingers get stained with cotton candy. I live here all year and don't want to be anywhere else, but particularly the week of Frederick-Fest…it just feels like home."

A shadow passed over his expression, and she regretted her sentimentality. Had she made him feel like an outsider, reminded him his own past wasn't quite as idyllic? It was true that Grace's past few years—with her father's death, Colleen's illness and the restaurant's decline—had been difficult. But up until then, she'd led a fairly charmed life.

"Do you dance?" she asked suddenly. He might not welcome a sympathetic hug, but there were other ways to get her arms around him. "There's a polka band around the corner."

"Polka, huh? I've managed that once or twice. Lead the way."

En route, they passed a stall selling an assortment of quality and novelty hats. He slowed to pick up a plastic green leprechaun bowler and plop it on his head. "What do you think?"

What she thought was that he was still trying to cajole her out of a bad mood, and she adored his flippant nature. It was the perfect antidote to everything weighing on her.

"Not actually the best look for you." She laughed. She stood on tiptoe to swat aside the ludicrous cap, then surveyed the racks of merchandise. Her gaze landed on a cowboy hat. Every true Texan needed one. "Here, try this."

Obligingly he settled it on his head, then tipped it back with a finger to smile down at her. Those blue-gray eyes hit her full force, and her breath caught. Damn, he was a good-looking man. She hadn't realized just how close they were standing until that moment and it seemed like the most natural thing in the world to slide her hands around his waist and reach up to meet his kiss.

The first time he'd kissed her had been spontaneous and short-lived. They'd been under a strict deadline. Now, Ty explored her mouth as if he had all the time in the world and nowhere else he'd rather be. He teased her relentlessly, tracing her lips without deepening the kiss. When he finally touched his tongue to hers, sharp, sweet pleasure pierced her.

"Graciela? *Dios mio,* you're in a public place, child!"

Grace jerked away from Ty so forcefully she almost knocked over a hat stand—which reminded her. "Give me that." She took back the cowboy hat, stalling while she tried to figure out how to face her aunt. "You can't be trusted to use this hat's power for good instead of evil."

"Are you kidding?" Ty whispered. "That was *very* good."

"Young man," Maria said imperiously. "Can you explain to me who you are and what you were doing with my niece?"

He looked down at the wizened woman who'd made lesser men tremble with her stony glare and promptly threw Grace under the bus. "I apologize, ma'am. But she started it."

That surprised a snort of laughter out of the septuagenarian. She quickly squelched it, but humor crinkled the corners of her eyes. "Irreverent cuss."

He gave her a beatific smile. "Yes, ma'am."

Grace stepped in. "Ty, this is my aunt. *Tía* Maria, this is Chef Ty Beckett. He's in town for the cooking competition, the one that's being filmed for TV?"

Maria frowned. "The two of you are…" She paused, searching for the word she wanted. "Adversaries?"

"In a manner of speaking," Grace said.

Maria pursed her lips. "Well, I suppose no one can fault your good sportsmanship."

Grace craned her neck to examine nearby booths and tents, trying to spot her mother in the crowd. "Did Victor bring you with Mom?"

"No." Sadness muted Maria's lively gaze. "She was having one of her bad days. He decided to stay with her and spend a calm afternoon together. I came with a couple of old friends. We were over there taste-testing jams when I saw you making a spectacle of yourself."

Ty put an arm around Grace's shoulder in a pleasantly protective gesture. "It won't happen again."

"Ha! Do I look foolish enough to trust a man like you?" But Maria said it with fondness, sounding much the way she did whenever she scolded her beloved nephews. "I have to catch up with my friends or those two biddies will finish all the good gossip without me. Try to behave yourselves!"

"Yes, ma'am," they chorused, causing Grace to erupt in giggles.

Her aunt tossed her hands in the air and walked away.

"I thought she was going to ground you," Ty said near her ear.

"Just be glad she didn't have her walking stick with her today. She might've knee-capped you."

"Nah. She liked me."

He was right about that. Grace put her hands on her hips, shaking her head in pseudo-exasperation. "Is there any woman you can't win over?"

"I don't know. But there's only one I want to win."

Done.

As SHE'D PONDERED DOING hours earlier, Grace leaned over and placed her head on Ty's shoulder. His arm was around her, and the view of the sunset from the Ferris wheel was lovely.

"You saved today for me," she confessed, nuzzling closer as they descended back to the ground. "My family always had a lot of fun on St. Patrick's Day, and this one got off to a really lousy start. I owe you."

"You make me sound nicer than I am," he protested. "This was completely selfish on my part. I— Hot damn, that's Bernie Dickinson! Stephen and I have been trying to get him on board for weeks. Son of a gun's hard to pin down. I have to get off this thing!"

"On board for what?" she asked. But Ty hardly seemed to hear her as he tugged impatiently at their seat belt.

"I'll be right back," Ty promised. "Wait for me? Look, there's a cotton-candy stand over there. Be back soon!" He thrust a five-dollar bill at her and loped off through the crowd.

So much for their peaceful, romantic interlude. She shouldn't be surprised, though. Ty had never made any secret of being ambitious. She didn't know who Bernie Dickinson was, but apparently Ty and his business manager needed him for something. Therefore, Bernie was about to experience the Ty Beckett full-court press. No one else she'd ever known was as successful at schmoozing. While it was borderline insulting to be ditched by the cotton-candy machine, she couldn't entirely blame him. If there was someone here who could magically save her restaurant, wouldn't she have chased him down just as eagerly?

In line for cotton candy, she exchanged greetings and small talk with people she knew. Afterward, she sat on a nearby bench. She'd eaten more than a quarter of the multicolored spun sugar puff when Ty returned, looking smug.

"And they say *I* don't have a poker face," she ridiculed. "Are you familiar with the expression 'cat who ate the canary'?"

Ty smirked. "By the way, Bernie said he went by the *Road Trip* pavilion earlier today and the tasting samples were going fast. Except for the potato foam."

Having satisfied her annual craving, she passed Ty the cotton candy. "So, who was that guy? Some sort of TV executive who oversees culinary programming?" She knew how much Ty's possible show meant to him.

"TV?" He gave her a chiding look. "You thought I ditched you to chat about cable opportunities?"

"Um…no?" she backpedaled. How was she supposed to know what other irons he had in the fire?

"He's the CEO of a statewide grocery chain." Ty scrubbed a hand over his jaw, looking self-conscious. "He voiced a passing interest in helping a food-related charity, but Stephen and I have been trying to get a firm commitment."

"Is this a charity you happen to support personally, or are you about to be unveiled as the new spokesperson of some group?" *Talk about using his powers for good.* She could imagine him charming plenty of people into writing very large checks.

"Spokesperson?" He grimaced, shaking his head. "I'll be remaining strictly behind the scenes."

Mr. Limelight, behind the scenes? "That doesn't sound like you." She crossed her arms over her chest, waiting. It was a technique she'd learned from her mother. Colleen had often had more success getting information from the men in her life by biding her time than asking direct questions.

"This isn't something I discuss with many people," Ty said.

"You seemed pretty anxious to discuss it with Bernie."

He sighed. "If I tell you, can I trust you not to out me?"

She nodded, highly intrigued.

"I'm putting together a charitable foundation whose mission is to get impoverished children fresh food," he explained. "Obviously it's easier to supply and ship canned goods and boxed meals, but—"

"You're embarrassed to talk about *that?* Why? It sounds like a wonderful initiative!" Comprehension dawned. "It's because you don't want anyone to make the connection, isn't it? You can't stand the idea of people finding out you were one of those impoverished children."

"It's not a deep dark secret, it's just not relevant. Nathan Tyler Beckett's past has nothing to do with Ty Beckett today."

That was such a staggering falsehood that for a second she couldn't form words. He couldn't possibly be deluded enough to believe what he was saying! She bit her tongue. He'd shared something he was sensitive about, and she wouldn't repay his confidence in her by arguing. "Your first name's Nathan?"

"Yeah. Very few people know that." He gave her a crooked smile. "Welcome to the inner circle."

She grinned. "I'm honored to be here."

Buzzing came from his pocket, and Ty took out his cell phone. "It's Stephen. Do you mind if I take this?"

"Go right ahead." She wiggled her sugarcoated fingers. "I need to wash my hands anyway."

As she navigated the crowd, she mulled over the paradox that a man who presented himself as so cocky could be so insecure. He seemed truly afraid of his past, as if it had the power to reclaim him. Didn't he realize it was a source of strength, that it had imbued him with so much determination? He should wear it like a badge of honor. She recalled Natalie's mournful assessment of Victor. *"He's teaching our children not to dream."*

Ty could be an inspiration to children who needed dreams. It wasn't only his past he tried to hide. He seemed equally discomfited by anyone seeing his generosity. Any time she thanked him for being kind, he seemed unequipped to handle the gratitude, usually joking about his ulterior motives. Her first impression of him, as a one-dimensional charmer, had been so very wrong. But he actively cultivated that image. Did he want people to think of him as lovably obnoxious and never look any deeper?

She pulled open the door to the ladies' room and found Lorelei Keller inside, brushing her long hair in front of the mirrors. "Hi again."

The tall brunette turned. "Grace! Nice to see you. Having a good time?"

Nodding, Grace stuck her hand under the soap dispenser. "You?"

Lorelei lowered her gaze. "Better than I expected. I haven't been to one of these in years. I wish I'd come back sooner."

"You here with Sam?" Grace glanced back to check for feet under stalls. She didn't want to unintentionally start rumors about anyone else's love life. "Not to put you on the spot, but the way he was looking at you Wednesday night? *Whew.* Half the women in the restaurant wanted to be in your place."

Lorelei smiled shyly. "The way he was looking at me, huh? Sometimes I think I see it, other times I wonder if it's all in my head."

"Not unless we were sharing a collective hallucination," Grace teased. "But I know what you mean. Men are tricky to read."

"I took combinatorial-mathematics courses at an Ivy League college, and they were easier to decipher than Sam Travis."

"But you like him anyway. Right?"

"Did Tess Fitzpatrick put you up to a fact-finding mission?" Lorelei asked suspiciously. "She's been driving me crazy about this all day."

"Sorry." Grace rinsed her hands. "I was being nosy. But on my own impulse. Tess had nothing to do with it, I promise."

"Well, you're right. I do like him," Lorelei admitted. "We have no future, though. We're both just passing through Fredericksburg and we're really different people. Tess advocates a fling, but… Could you get involved with someone, someone you're really starting to care about, even if you knew it wouldn't last?"

The flaw in Lorelei's reasoning was the assumption that *anything* lasted. No one had expected Grace's father to die when he had, leaving Colleen alone. But at least they'd had decades together—Victor and Natalie's marriage had been far shorter. Grace had grown up believing a Torres would always run The Twisted Jalapeño. Would that truism prove a myth? Another constant had been her parents' unconditional love, yet now she had to accept there might come a day when her mother didn't even know her.

"Life is unpredictable." Her throat tightened. "If it were me—if there was a guy I cared about and we shared a mutual attraction—I'd go for it. Enjoy whatever time you have while you have it."

She glanced at the mirror, meeting her gaze in the reflection, and wondered: was she brazen enough to take her own advice?

Chapter Nine

"Thanks, Rosie." Grace smiled at the employee who'd given Ty and Grace a quick lift back to where Grace's car was parked.

"Sure thing, boss." The words may have been directed at Grace, but the young woman's gaze was locked on Ty.

Grace inwardly rolled her eyes, not really blaming Rosie for the infatuated way she'd been looking at him. *How could I fault her?* Grace was more than a little infatuated herself.

Keys in hand, she walked toward her car.

Ty fell into step with her. "You're sure you don't mind joining us for dinner?" His earlier phone call had been Stephen Zigler saying he and his wife were on their way into Fredericksburg. "Don't get me wrong, I'd love to have you there. But you've already had a long day."

She pretended to give the matter serious consideration as she opened her door. "Well, putting up with you *was* pretty taxing, but I think I can muster one last burst of energy."

"Smart-ass." He slid into the passenger seat. "I know it can be daunting to be the new person in a group where everyone else has history together, but take my word for it, Donna is going to love you."

"Actually, it sounds like a novel experience." Having

grown up in the same place her entire life, blessed with such welcoming, socially active parents, Grace had never really been the new person. "Do you get intimidated in group settings where you're the new guy?"

"On the contrary. That's where I shine. When people first meet, the relationship's a clean slate. No one has any reason to feel bitter or let down—it's all wide-open potential." He gave her a wry smile. "I can be very dazzling in the short-term."

"Maybe if you gave yourself the chance, you could be equally dazzling in the long run." As soon as she said it, she realized it wasn't quite the point she'd wanted to make. When you had people in your life who loved and accepted you, it wasn't necessary to be dazzling all the time. She didn't have to be the most charming version of herself 24/7. Amy would continue to be her friend even if Grace had a seriously cranky PMS day, and she was pretty sure *Tía* Maria still loved her, despite Grace's lusty display in front of the festival's hat shack.

From the restaurant where they'd started the day, the drive to Grace's apartment took only a few minutes. After she'd helped Ty and the Ziglers choose a place to eat, her first thought had been to drop Ty off so he could change, run home herself, then pick him up again. But they'd decided it would be more expedient to simply wait for each other while the other one quickly freshened up. As she unlocked her front door, she realized Ty was the only guy who'd been in the apartment since she and Jeff had broken up over a month ago.

"Colorful," he quipped when they stepped inside. "Looks like you apply your fusion approach to decorating, too."

"Amy and I were compensating for the size. We can't

do anything to make it bigger, but we can certainly make it brighter."

"Job well done."

There wasn't anything particularly loud or busy in the living room decor—the wildest they'd gone were some cow-print accents in the kitchen—but it wasn't demure, either. A leather love seat and a neutral-colored futon in a wrought-iron frame were piled with throw pillows in different sizes, textures and solid colors. The multihued geometric-print throw rug tied the colors together. The back wall was covered in a mishmash of offbeat artwork, photos and framed menus.

She pointed him toward the couch and dug the remote control out from beneath a cooking magazine. "Want a bottle of water or cold beer while you wait?"

He shook his head, then smiled. "Want any help undressing? I could be helpful with buttons and hooks."

"I'll bet. You, sit. I'll give a shout if I run across anything that needs your expertise."

He held up crossed fingers, and she laughed all the way down the hall.

Inside her room, however, she cringed—definitely no way she would bring a man here. *Gracie, this place is a mess.* The bed was unmade, and the carpet had forgotten what a vacuum cleaner looked like. She'd washed clothes, but she hadn't exactly been folding them or putting them away. They spilled across the cedar chest her father had refinished for her when she was a teen. Makeup and jewelry were jumbled haphazardly atop her vanity. She'd been so upset with her brothers when she woke that morning—feeling angry and powerless and hurt—that she'd rummaged through her accessories, trying to find some miraculous combination that would empower her. In the end, she'd given up and gone with a minimalist look.

Ty certainly hadn't complained, she thought with a smile. Ever since their kiss this afternoon, he hadn't been able to keep his hands off her. He hadn't been pushy or made her uncomfortable. He'd simply made her feel wanted.

Pulling a yellow slip dress off a hanger in her closet, she recalled her advice to Lorelei. *Go for it.* Biting her lip, Grace made a quick detour toward her lingerie drawer and swapped out the perfectly serviceable bra-and-panties set she was wearing for something a bit more delicate. Just in case. Then she pulled the dress over her head, slid her feet into a pair of sandals, shook out her hair and dabbed on some shiny lip gloss. She grabbed a muted yellow-and-green loose-weave sweater on her way out of the room.

"Ready," she announced.

Ty raised his eyebrows. "Wow. How'd you manage a transformation that fast?"

"I can get in and out of clothes very quickly," she drawled.

He swallowed. "Good to know."

As they drove back to his hotel, Grace said, "I've been wondering…would you tell me how you became a chef? You're young to have accomplished so much."

He slanted her a glance she couldn't read in the dark. "This from a woman in her mid-twenties who runs a restaurant? Trust me, sweetheart, between the two of us, you've got the tougher job. I've gained myself some attention because I'm good with sound bites."

"It's because you're good with food. Don't diminish yourself."

"I convinced a diner owner to let me bus tables part-time while I was in high school. Luanne Bauer, God bless her. Pay wasn't much, but she let me have any bad orders that were caught before they left the kitchen—entrées a bit too burned to serve, scrambled eggs that were supposed to have been over easy. The diner food was better than anything at home, but not as good as what some of my friends ate, especially Tony Harding. I told Tony's mom I wanted to make a romantic dinner for a girl and asked her to show me some tricks. I took a cooking elective at school, looked up as much as I could on the library computer. When Luanne fired the short-order cook for stealing, I sweet-talked her into giving me a shot even though I wasn't technically old enough. She said it was temporary, until she found a replacement."

"And how long did that take?" Grace asked, betting that once he had his foot in the door, he'd been able to alternately charm and impress his employer into letting him keep the job.

"Held that position until I was seventeen. As long as no one complained, Luanne let me improvise with the recipes. And then I got lucky. There was a restaurant owner from another county who drove through a few times a year to visit her sister in McAllen. Since we were one of the few restaurants on that stretch of the highway open late, she got stuck eating at Luanne's. On one of her trips, she asked to see me. I thought I'd done something wrong. She'd noticed a difference in the food and was curious about the person responsible."

"The first time someone asked to pay their compliments to the chef, huh?" And he'd been seventeen. Grace couldn't help being proud on his behalf.

"It's happened plenty of times since, but that one's still my favorite," he said. "She asked a bunch of questions and when she was satisfied I knew my stuff, she handed me her business card and told me that if I ever relocated farther north, she had an opening for a line cook. I was legally old enough to leave home, so I did. I made friends fast and slept on couches until I could afford to split rent with a couple of waiters."

He fell silent, and Grace assumed they'd reached the end of the story.

But then he added, "I left my mom and Luanne behind. I got my GED and after six months at the new restaurant, making connections in a much richer culinary environment, I moved on again. I found an employer willing to help pay for some classes. My career's been like a big game of leapfrog. Seize an opportunity, make the most of it while I'm there, figure out who to impress to take the next step and upgrade to something better."

Which brought them to the present. This competition in Fredericksburg was another opportunity for him, another step toward something bigger. He'd leave without a second glance. That was his pattern.

She didn't begrudge him his progress—this man owed her nothing and had never made any false promises. She refused to feel sorry for herself when he'd gone. The person she felt bad for was *him,* always bouncing, never landing for long, trying to escape his past once and for all. She didn't have the heart to point out that it was physically impossible to outrun yourself.

They walked into his hotel together. "Would you be more comfortable waiting in my room, or the lobby lounge?" Ty asked.

"I'll come up, if you don't mind." If anyone connected with *Road Trip* passed by, she'd rather they didn't know she was out with Ty tonight. Whatever happened between them, it was personal, not reality-show fodder.

Ever the gentleman, he opened the door for her. At her apartment, he'd gotten a glimpse of where she lived and what she was like. She didn't have the same chance to see his private world. There was only generic hotel artwork and evidence of a scrupulous housekeeping staff.

"Where do you live full-time?" she wanted to know.

"I have a cheap and depressing efficiency apartment in the Dallas Fort Worth area," he said, "but I'm rarely there. I'm saving up for something special, wherever I finally settle. I've done some work with resort restaurants where they let me use unoccupied rooms. Donna and Stephen have put me up more times than I can count."

He took a change of clothes into the bathroom, then called through the door. "I'm lucky—Donna once said I remind her of a chocolate lab her family adopted when she was a kid. She's got a soft spot for me. And I travel enough that I've met lots of people."

"So you can call them up and crash on their couches if need be?"

"Something like that."

It took him even less time to get ready than it had her, so they were back on the road within minutes.

"Perfect timing," Ty said as she pulled into the lot of a quaint but high-quality steak house. "That's Stephen's car." Because so many people were enjoying evening activities at Frederick-Fest, the restaurant's parking lot was largely empty.

They waited on the curb while Stephen helped his wife out of the car. With her pale coloring and pixie features, she managed to look heavily pregnant yet delicate at the same time.

She's no taller than I am, Grace realized as the woman waddled up the sidewalk. "I like her already."

The feeling was obviously mutual. Donna beamed at her. "You must be Grace! Oh, I've heard *all* about you. I'd hug you, but—" She patted her stomach. "The watermelon gets in the way."

"I'll hug her for both of us," Stephen declared, side-stepping Ty.

Even with the advance notice, Grace was still a little surprised when Ty's business manager pulled her into an affectionate embrace.

In a fake whisper, Stephen asked, "Is he driving you crazy? We really appreciate your not running him out of town."

"Well, not *yet*," Grace deadpanned. "I make no promises for the future."

She was taking a page out of Ty's book. For now, all she wanted to think about was the present.

THE FOUR OF THEM SHARED a wonderfully mellow meal, aided by a bottle of red wine that caused Donna to pout comically. As Grace sat cozied up to Ty on their side of the booth, she realized this was the most relaxed she'd felt since… She tried to recall a time in recent memory when she'd let her troubles go. She didn't want the night to end, but Donna was clearly drooping.

"Being seven months pregnant isn't as easy as it looks," the blonde said around a yawn. "And for some weird reason, sitting in a car for a few hours can really take it out of you. Makes no sense."

"You should tuck Donna in for the night," Ty told his friend. "I'll wait for the check. Grace and I might even split dessert."

"Good plan," Stephen agreed. "Oh, but before I forget, here. This might help cover the cost." He pushed an envelope across the table.

Ty frowned. "I told you earlier this was my treat. I don't want your money."

"It's, uh, your money. Beth sent me a letter and a reimbursement of the last check."

Beth? Even though she knew she was being inexcusably nosy, Grace used her peripheral vision to get a quick peek at the return address. Beth Beckett. Roja, Texas.

"She says she doesn't want any more of your financial assistance," Stephen was saying. "All she's ever wanted—"

"That's a discussion for later," Ty interrupted, his voice clipped. He shoved the envelope back at Stephen with a tight smile. "We're being completely insensitive to your wife."

"So we are. How thoughtful of you," Stephen said dryly.

Donna jabbed her husband in the shoulder and whispered something not audible from the other side of the table. But Grace bet it was along the lines of "play nice."

After the Ziglers left, Ty's posture relaxed again. He grinned down at Grace. "That went according to my nefarious plan. I was afraid if I didn't get rid of the Ziglers, Stephen would offer to give me a lift back to the hotel so you could go straight home." With grudging chivalry, he added, "We *do* have another big day tomorrow. If you want to ditch me here, I can get a cab."

She shook her head. "I'm not ready for the evening to be over, either."

Nor was she feeling as tranquil as she had a moment ago. Her cells started to buzz with awareness. Now that the Ziglers had cleared out, their candlelit booth in the back of the restaurant, the heat of Ty's body against hers, had taken on a much more intimate feel.

Grace swirled the last of her wine around in her glass. "Can I ask you a personal question? You haven't ever... been married, have you?"

"Like anyone would have me!" he teased. "No. I've never married."

Beth Beckett definitely wasn't an ex-wife, then. *His*

mother. That's what her intuition told her. Had he been sending her money this entire time?

"You want any dessert?" Ty asked. "Maybe a cocktail, cup of coffee?"

She looked him dead in the eye. "No."

He traced his thumb over her jawline, coming to a stop right below her mouth. "Want to get out of here?"

"Yes."

He paid the bill in a hurry. The night air was easily fifteen degrees cooler than it had been during the day. With a shiver, she snuggled closer to Ty.

"Can I drive?" he asked.

"Just this once." She felt shaky. Not in a bad way, but how she used to feel at the top of the first hill of a giant roller coaster—before they shot past the point of no return and her pulse pounded and her soul soared and all she could think was *again, again, again.* Her brothers had always been suitably impressed when it came to her theme-park daredevil streak. At the time, she hadn't been able to imagine any greater thrill. Now she could.

"So if I asked you for details on your memorable trip to New Orleans," he began coaxingly.

"Nice try." She changed the subject. "Were you serious this morning when you said you wanted to cook for me sometime?"

"Name the time and the place."

None of her boyfriends had ever cooked for her. "It's intimidating enough trying to pick a restaurant," one had complained. It made her feel pampered to think of Ty preparing food for her. It also felt intensely personal, which she supposed was silly since both of them cooked for huge groups and total strangers all the time. But she'd grown up in a house where food had been a way of expressing love. He'd missed out on that. Suddenly she wished she'd had the idea first, to cook for him.

When they finally pulled into the parking lot of the hotel, he asked, "Would you like to come up?" The question was only a formality. After their kiss today and the building tension ever since, there was no question how this night would end.

She gave him the most innocent smile she could muster. "Unless you wanted to make love right here in the car."

When his jaw dropped, she laughed out loud.

"Go easy on me," he reproached. "I still have to make it through the lobby."

Hands interlocked, they raced to the elevators with their heads lowered as if that would fool anyone who saw them—him having a nearly famous face, and her being a very distinctive height.

Just inside the door of his room, he hit a button and every light in his suite came on. "Not the most romantic lighting, is it?"

"Not really." She draped her discarded sweater on the back of a chair, then kicked off her shoes.

Ty did the same as he dimmed the bedside lamp by the king bed. He turned off all the other lights except for the one in the entryway. It was dark enough to provide atmosphere but still plenty bright enough for her to enjoy the sight of him.

He held out a hand in silent invitation, and she let him pull her into his arms. His lips captured hers in a tantalizing kiss that made her think of roller coasters again—vivid loop-the-loops, illuminated by fireworks overhead.

She nibbled at the skin exposed in the vee of his unbuttoned collar. "By any chance," she said between soft bites, "do you like roller coasters?"

He speared a hand through her hair, tilting her head back so he could kiss her again. "Love them. Why?"

But he got distracted and didn't seem to mind when she never answered. She helped him out of his shirt, lightly trailing her fingertips over his chest. He wasn't quite as gentle. He cupped one breast through her clothes and stroked his thumb firmly over one rigid nipple. Grace gasped. He elicited another shuddery inhalation when he reached for the hem of her dress and lifted. She raised her arms above her head, feeling deliciously wanton when she stood before him in the lace-trimmed satin lingerie.

"So beautiful." The huskiness in his voice made him sound almost harsh, so unlike his usual suave manner that it was a compliment in itself. He ran his hands over the small of her back, down to the silky material covering her butt. He rocked her against his erection in time with their kisses, and she moaned, erotic anticipation coiling tighter and tighter inside.

He backed her toward the bed and when her legs hit the mattress, they tumbled together. He caught himself so he didn't crush her with his weight, but she reveled in the feel of him atop her. Before she'd met Ty in person, she'd once questioned his attention span, knowing it took great patience to be a great chef. Forty minutes after they fell across the bed, she could attest that Ty had enough patience to be the best. He'd stroked and kissed all over her body and she burned with need.

Impatient for him to fill her, to finally send her hurtling over that edge, she used her smaller size to shimmy free, then rolled him onto his back. She straddled him, her smile wicked as she took what she wanted, lowering herself on him in exquisite degrees. A tidal wave of sensation crashed over her as he gripped her hips and thrust inside her. Her climax rippled through her, gaining force, going on and on, until she lay completely boneless in his arms.

"Grace," he whispered. There was a wealth of emotion in that single syllable.

She nodded against his chest. "I know. Me, too."

WRAPPED IN ONE OF THE FLUFFY white hotel towels, Grace stomped across Ty's hotel room. "I can't believe I'm doing the walk of shame *on television!*"

Ty propped himself on one elbow, enjoying the sight of her too much to get out of bed. "You'll have on a chef's jacket on TV. And no one knows you wore that dress for a couple of hours. Last time anyone from the show saw you, you had on a tank top and jeans."

"At least the front desk sent me up a toothbrush," she muttered. "But I should have left when I suggested it at midnight." She fixed him with a rebuking stare. "Remind me again why I didn't go."

He grinned lazily, content all the way to his toes. "For the same reason you didn't go at two-thirty or five o'clock this morning?"

"I blame you." But she wasn't fooling anyone; an irrepressible smile tugged at her mouth.

She turned toward the bathroom with her armful of clothes but whirled back to drop one last kiss on his lips. Then she was gone. Seconds later he heard the hair dryer droning in the next room. He stared up at the ceiling, wondering what good thing he'd ever done to deserve last night. *And this morning.*

He'd always kidded Grace about how expressive she was, but honestly, he was worried about how *he'd* do today. If he glanced her way in the kitchen, would people see the naked adoration on his face? She'd decimated him last night, destroyed him completely. Around three in the morning, he'd found himself wondering whether those brothers of hers would actually sell the Jalapeño, and, if so, how the cable network might feel about the idea of a stunning female co-host. That was groundbreaking for him. He'd never been comfortable having any kind of partner, professionally or personally. It had taken a long time for his friendship with Stephen to develop into anything more reciprocal than Ty paying the money and giving the orders.

The fleeting co-host idea was nothing more than a sleep-deprived flight of fancy, of course. He hadn't even sold the network on the idea of *him*. He wouldn't rock the boat and jeopardize all he'd worked for by making a suggestion that would increase their expenses. Besides, he doubted very much Grace would be happy with that kind of job. He remembered the bewilderment in her eyes when she'd asked why he'd never opened his own place, made his mark.

Because when you make your mark in just one place, it can be taken away from you—as he was afraid she was about to learn with her restaurant. Ty didn't want to invest all his energy in one venture. He needed to have his fingers in multiple pies so he knew there'd always be enough.

He halfheartedly told himself that maybe after this, he could come back to Fredericksburg and visit. But Grace was a special woman. She deserved far more than glorified booty calls. Besides, as much as he was trying not to think it, once this competition had played out, she may not want to see him again. Ty had mastered the art of the short-term relationship and inevitable goodbye. But never had he felt so desperate to squeeze in every possible second with someone while he still could.

He'd spent his adult life moving on—from relationships, restaurants, cities. But the Beckett Instinct was telling him, next time he moved on, it wouldn't be a clean getaway. This time, he'd leave part of himself behind.

THE COOKING CHALLENGE ON Sunday turned out to be a chili cook-off, which Grace should have guessed, given that there had always been some form of the event at the festival.

"After all the beer I saw yesterday," Reed joked as he crossed the kitchen, "I thought maybe our assignment would be to create the most effective hangover remedy."

Jo groaned. She was standing in front of a cutting board but had yet to pick up a knife. Instead she leaned against the counter with a bag of ice pressed to her head. "I could use some of that. I ended up in a lengthy discussion with a vintner who was generous with his tasting samples. And then last night I tried three different kinds of margaritas at Grace's restaurant."

Katharine looked up from the large pot she was stirring. "We dropped by to say hi and check out your place," she told Grace. "But you weren't there. Sorry we missed you."

Grace felt the heat climbing in her cheeks. *Whatever you do, don't look at Ty!* She wanted to, though. Looking at him had become one of her favorite pastimes, right up there with cooking. That smile of his was addictive—to say nothing of his kisses.

"I, uh, wasn't there," she stammered.

Katharine laughed, her expression puzzled. "We know. I just said that, remember? I'm still glad we stopped in. To tell you the truth, the restaurant isn't much to look at, but the appetizers we shared were wonderful."

"Thank you." The praise was bittersweet. An acclaimed executive chef with experience all over the country, as well as a woman Grace personally admired, had just paid her a compliment, but she couldn't truly savor it. By the time Frederick-Fest happened again next March, would the Jalapeño even be in business?

It will be if I have anything to say about it.

Tonight was Sunday dinner, a Torres tradition that dated back to Grace's childhood. After church, there'd be a light lunch, followed by some group activity—hiking, fishing, window shopping at local antique stores. Then the entire family would chip in to help make an early supper before Victor Senior went to work at the Jalapeño for the evening. Now, of course, their weekly meal took place in the dining room of Gunther Gardens, but all three Torres siblings were there at 4:00 p.m. every Sunday.

Which meant Grace's brothers couldn't hide from her. Though she would have to be careful not to agitate their mom, Grace didn't plan to let Ben or Victor off the hook. *Brace yourselves, boys. There's a reckoning coming.*

Chapter Ten

Since the chefs didn't have to be back at the *Road Trip* pavilion until three for the ruling on the crowd's favorite chili, Grace and Ty had been wandering the festival with the Ziglers. Currently Grace kept Donna company in front of a stage while the men went to get cold refreshments. It was unseasonably warm, and Grace could only imagine how much hotter it felt for her pregnant friend.

"If you want, we can move to that bench over there," Grace offered. "It's better shaded."

Donna glanced to where Grace was pointing. "Yeah, but it doesn't have as good a view. And this is the cutest show ever!" A group of preschool-age tap dancers in bright yellow tutus were doing a number to "Deep in the Heart of Texas." What they lacked in choreographic proficiency, they made up for with sheer enthusiasm.

From Grace's vantage point, she also had a highly entertaining view of Tess Fitzpatrick standing offstage, going through the motions for any little dancers who forgot the steps. Beneath the music coming through the speakers, the rhythmic clapping in the chorus and the metallic taps of twenty little shoes, Grace gradually became aware of muffled sniffling.

"Donna? You okay?"

Her friend pulled a tissue out of her purse, dabbing

at her eyes. "Fine. I just... Ever since I reached my third trimester, whenever I see adorable little kids, I... Oh, for Pete's sake!"

Grace chuckled. "You don't have to be embarrassed in front of me. I once cried over a soup commercial, and I didn't even have pregnancy hormones to blame."

"If we have a girl, I hope she's as adorable as these." The other night, Donna had mentioned that she and Stephen had opted to be surprised by the baby's gender. They'd gone with a brightly colored teddy bear theme in the nursery and had been stocking up on lots of neutral green and yellow onesies and baby blankets.

"Is that what you're hoping for?" Grace asked. "A little girl?"

"I'll be thrilled either way, but sometimes, I kind of hope it's a boy. I have all these daydreams about watching Stephen with our son—throwing a football for the first time or taking him to Scout meetings. How cute our kid would look in his little uniform." She broke off with a hiccup. "Sorry. The hormones are *really* out of control today. Can I tell you a secret?"

"Absolutely." Grace was honored Donna would trust her with something personal, considering how short a time they'd known each other. But she loved the Ziglers. It warmed her heart to think that, despite not having much family or a home of his own, Ty had them in his life.

"He doesn't know it yet, but if we have a boy, we're naming him after Ty."

Which name? Grace wondered. Tyler or Nathan? Either was great, but it truly disturbed her how much he wanted to deny his past. If you spent year upon year trying to erase who you'd been, how did you know who you were?

Grace looked around, doing a quick check of the stage area to make sure the men weren't back yet. "Donna, that money Stephen tried to give Ty last night? That was from his mother, wasn't it?"

Donna nodded glumly. "The situation is such a shame. He doesn't talk about her, but he has Stephen cut her checks. For the last two years Stephen's also snuck in newspaper clippings and magazine articles. We thought she might be interested in following her son's career, if only from a distance. To the best of my knowledge, she's never tried to contact him directly, which I do not get. If it were *my* child…" she began, sounding fiercely protective. Then she gave herself a little shake, regaining her composure. "They're both at fault. She's his mama. Ty should visit her sometime. At least pick up the darn phone on Mother's Day! I guess she cashed the latest check but thought better of keeping it. She sent Stephen the money and told him she won't take any more. All she wants is to hear from her son."

Then Beth Beckett had a long, futile wait ahead of her. Grace cared deeply for Ty, might even lo—*don't think it.* The *Road Trip* winner would be announced at the big festival dance this Friday, and then it would be goodbye. In the interest of self-preservation, she should try not to fall any harder for him than she already had. But the point was, as much as she liked and admired him, as much as she might *want* to believe he could prioritize repairing a personal relationship above outrunning his past—

"Híjole." Grace shot to her feet.

"Grace?" Donna sounded alarmed. "What is it?"

"Mis hermanos." She pointed toward a nearby picnic table where three men stood. "My treacherous, good-for-nothing brothers." And they'd cornered Ty.

AFTER WAITING IN LINE FOR nearly fifteen minutes, Stephen and Ty had finally reached the front, only to discover that the concession stand was out of ice.

"There's more coming," the apologetic woman working the register said. "It should be here any second. Right now, I've only got enough for one drink."

Stephen had sent Ty back with the single iced beverage for Donna. "I'll get one of those drinks carriers and bring the other three. Go ahead, you and Grace don't have much longer until judges' panel."

What he didn't mention was the slim chance that either Ty or Grace could be voted out this afternoon. *Not gonna happen.* She was a terrific chef who probably understood local palates better than anyone. And he'd overheard enough snatches of conversation to know his grilled corned beef had been a hit with this Texas crowd. Still, he felt compelled to take advantage of as many carefree festival moments with her as possible before today's elimination announcement.

So he'd headed back to where they'd left the ladies waiting. The last thing he'd expected was for two men to step into his path. He recognized one as Officer Ben from yesterday. He assumed the other one was Grace's second brother since both men had the same basic look—tall, dark and ticked off.

Two things struck him as curious: that diminutive Grace would have brothers as tall as he was and that a man on crutches could still be reasonably intimidating.

"Afternoon, guys." He gave them a winning smile. Neither smiled in return. "Ben and I have already met. You must be...Vic?"

"Only to close friends and family," the older of the two snapped.

"What can I do for you gentlemen?" Ty asked. *Besides*

dump this drink over your collective heads and demand to know what the hell you think you're doing suggesting she sell that restaurant. These two clods had to know how important it was to Grace. Yet, judging by the overprotective way they'd tracked him down, they cared about her plenty.

Victor glowered. "It's not about us. It's what you should do for Grace."

Ben nodded vehemently. "She's well liked here. Everyone knows her and respects her. She doesn't need *you* messing up her reputation. If you cared about her at all, you wouldn't reduce her to a public spectacle."

Sparks of anger caught and ignited. Ty had been willing to let her big brothers make a fuss and be possessive, but they were skirting dangerously close to insulting. "Nobody 'reduces' Grace to anything. Watch it."

The Torres men exchanged startled glances. They apparently hadn't expected Ty to be so prickly about her. Frankly it was a novel experience. He primarily looked out for himself. He wasn't usually around long enough to care or get involved with other people's problems. *I'd be willing to stick up for Stephen if it was ever necessary— but Donna would beat me to it.*

Victor appeared to be the less irate of the two, which was like saying "the less poisonous" of two toxic death cap mushrooms. He raised his palms. "It must seem old-fashioned to ask what your intentions are, but are you stringing our sister along? I understand you're only in town until this weekend, at the latest."

It sucked, having the very thing you were trying not to think about pointed out to you by a self-righteous banker. "What's between me and Grace," he said calmly, "is between me and Grace. She knows my situation."

"Yeah, well, when you leave," Ben interjected, making

it sound as if Ty couldn't get out of town soon enough, "she'll eventually start dating someone here. Someone she might marry and have kids with. She doesn't need—"

An explosion of rapid-fire words interrupted. The stream of dialogue was so fast that, at first, Ty couldn't make out individual words. But then his ears adjusted.

"—think you are? What, have you been *stalking* him?" Grace demanded, advancing on her brothers. "Hiding behind trees, just waiting for a chance to get him alone? Do I interfere in your love lives? No! Victor, I've stood by you during this idiotic divorce process, even though, after talking to Nat the other day—"

"You spoke to her?" The man's voice was a painful mix of anxiety and yearning. "Did she—"

"Not the point!" Grace blasted. "This running off any guy who might be interested in me got old in middle school. Leave Ty alone."

"We're looking out for you," Ben said. "Lots of people saw you together, all over the festival the other day. Making out."

She rolled her eyes. "Like there weren't a hundred other couples doing the same thing all over town? I kissed my date. I wasn't doing a striptease."

"Grace!" This from all three men.

"We don't want to see you hurt," Victor said. As attempted mollification, it completely backfired.

"Don't want to see me…" Her eyes were the size of dinner plates. "You…"

Here it comes, Ty thought, *the very loud Spanish.* But he couldn't have been more wrong. Her voice dropped so low they had to lean closer to catch her words.

"Explain how you think *he* could possibly hurt me more than *you* already have." She turned on her heel and stormed away.

Victor hung his head, looking so miserable Ty almost pitied him. Ben stared after her as if debating whether to follow.

"I wouldn't," Ty advised. "She's really upset. You should have seen her when she came into the challenge kitchen yesterday. The two of you almost destroyed her chances of winning this. Or is that what you wanted? To sabotage her, so she'd have to sell?"

"Of course not!" Victor looked appalled. "She works so hard, considers herself personally responsible for all the employees there. Everything with our parents has already taken a toll on her. I don't want that restaurant to be her albatross. You don't understand."

"Maybe not," Ty allowed. "But I've only known her a week. For people who've known her a lifetime, you've made a mess of things."

With that, he chased after Grace. Whatever happened in judging today, he didn't want her to face it in this frame of mind. She deserved better.

She deserves better than you. The thought sliced through him. Her brothers were a couple of misguided chuckleheads who apparently hadn't gotten the memo that Grace was all grown up and could make her own choices—but they were right that Ty would be leaving. Was he being selfish, spending all this time with her when they had no future?

A moot point. Because he just wasn't altruistic enough to quit.

THE PAVILION HAD BEEN temporarily closed to the public, and the five remaining chefs stood awaiting their fates. Grace wished she could squeeze Ty's hand for luck and moral support, but it was enough that he stood to her right, his nearness comforting. They hadn't arrived at the exact same time, but she didn't think they were fooling anyone. Reed had regarded her with raised eyebrows, and Jo had grinned and flashed a thumbs-up.

Damien thanked them all for their hard work so far and told them that they'd start with yesterday's placements. "As you know, in lieu of guest judges for this round, we decided to take it to the people and let them weigh in on who's the best. You've presented two dishes each, completely anonymous, and the public has spoken. Reed, your potato gnocchi yesterday was the clear loser. But, Jo, I'm afraid the crowd was also underwhelmed by your bread. Ty and Katharine, on the other hand, each made very favorable impressions. But the person with the most votes…was Grace Torres. Congratulations, Chef! Now, for today's results."

Grace balanced on the balls of her feet, springing slightly. The longer this competition went on, the more irritating she found their host's dramatic pauses. She was thrilled to have won yesterday's cook-off but anxious to hear her combined score.

"In an unexpected twist," Damien said, "Reed had the festivalgoers' favorite chili! From dead last, to number one."

Reed expelled a pent-up breath, looking pale but relieved. At least if he were sent home, he could retain some dignity.

"Katharine and Jo were the middle of the pack, with Ty and Grace tied for second place."

A tie? Her heart thumped. Too bad the overall competition couldn't end in a tie. Of course, she would have wished for *first* place.

"Grace, Ty, Katharine, you're all safe and will move on to our finals and the food demonstrations this week that will be covered by multiple culinary magazines. Enjoy the publicity and the chance to show Texas what you can do! Reed, Jo…for one of you the journey ends here. Jo, while you weren't dead last in either day's challenge, your scores all around were fairly lackluster. Reed, your phenomenal chili has saved you, allowing you to continue."

The chefs gathered around Jo to tell her how much she'd be missed and how much they respected her. Katharine invited her to visit New York and help revamp the dessert menu at Katharine's restaurant. Ty and Grace waited until judging was over and they'd had a chance to slip out before congratulating each other.

He scooped her into a quick hug, and her feet left the ground as he whirled her around. "First place yesterday! You worked hard to earn that."

She felt suddenly shy, ducking her head and tucking a strand of hair behind her ear. "We all worked hard. It could have just as easily been one of you."

He jabbed her in the shoulder. "Hey!" With a frown, he asked, "Who was it the other day telling *me* not to diminish myself?"

She couldn't help laughing. "All right, fine. I'm a big steaming pile of awesome. Happy?"

"Know what would make me truly happy? Let me buy you dinner somewhere to celebrate."

"I can't. It's Sunday."

"Which is a problem because…?"

"Family dinner." She checked her watch. "I have to run, or I'm going to be late." When she glanced up again, meeting his eyes, an idea struck. "Come with me."

His eyebrows shot so high NASA was probably tracking them. "Excuse me? Dinner with your family? Including two brothers who hate me?"

"And the aunt you made such an impression on yesterday," she said cheekily. Then she grew somber. "Plus my mother. Please, Ty. It would mean a lot to me for you to meet her."

"All right," he conceded. "For you."

They arrived at Gunther Gardens only a heartbeat before her brothers. Ben's indignant "What is *he* doing here?" reverberated through the lobby.

Grace spun, her voice a hiss. "So help me, if you don't behave yourself, I'll find a sympathetic nurse and have her sedate you! We are here for a nice family dinner, he is my guest and you are not going to cause trouble. *Comprendes?*"

Victor and Ben exchanged glances. It occurred to Grace belatedly that in the time she'd dated Jeff, she'd never once invited him to family dinner.

"If it means that much to you," Victor said softly. "Believe it or not, Graciela, we do want you to be happy."

His words twisted her insides, but she didn't want to have that conversation in the lobby where half a dozen people could overhear. The three Torres siblings decided it would be less disconcerting for Colleen to meet a new person if she wasn't surrounded by a crowd.

"You go and get Mom," Ben said. "We'll escort *Tía* Maria to the dining room and meet you there."

As they split down two separate corridors, Ty murmured, "I guess your brothers aren't completely awful."

She grinned wearily. "Not exactly high praise, but probably nicer than anything they've said about you so far."

"Well, they obviously love you. That's a redeeming quality."

When they reached her mother's apartment, Grace mentally crossed her fingers. She hoped Colleen was having a good night and wouldn't react badly to Ty's presence. Maybe it had been selfish to bring him here, but Grace wanted her mother to meet the man who'd come to mean so much to her. When Grace was a girl, she'd worn her hair superlong, "like Rapunzel," Colleen had teased; as she'd brushed Grace's hair each night, her mother told her one day she'd meet her prince. "Only he might not be a prince, exactly, so you have to look with your heart. He may be a fireman or a schoolteacher or a rancher."

Or an irreverent chef with a tendency to keep his eyes peeled for life's emergency exits?

The door to apartment 18 opened. Grace was relieved to see how animated her mom looked. She'd curled her hair, which fell in loose waves that made her look younger, and she wore makeup. The application was nearly perfect, except for a few smudges where the lipstick had missed her mouth.

That mouth pursed into a fretful scowl when she spotted Ty. "Oh, dear. Have we met? This is embarrassing," Colleen said, "because I can't recall—"

"No, ma'am," Ty interrupted. "I haven't had the pleasure. My name's Ty Beckett. I hope you don't mind my joining the dinner party."

"Ah, you're Maria's new beau!" Eyes sparkling, she turned to Grace, her voice dropping to a conspiratorial whisper. "He's dreamy, but you know your brother will give him the third degree." To Ty, she added, "My fiancé is the most darling man in the world, but possessive of his sister."

Maria? Fiancé? It took Grace a moment to wade through her mother's commentary. *She thinks I'm my aunt, decades ago.* In Colleen's mind, were they about to go on a double date? *Mom doesn't know me.*

Grace couldn't breathe. She was unaware that she'd gripped Ty's arm until he covered her hand with his own.

"Easy," he murmured. He smiled at Colleen. "You look lovely. Shall we go?"

"Shouldn't we wait for Victor?"

A few times before Colleen had moved into this apartment, she'd forgotten her husband was deceased. Grace had gently reminded her—each time as wrenching as the last—that Victor Senior was gone. Now she wasn't sure what to say. There were too many delusions to correct without upsetting her.

"We're supposed to meet at the restaurant," Grace finally said, the unshed tears in her eyes scalding hot. Her throat was raw and she tasted copper in her mouth. *Must've bitten my tongue.* She told herself she could get through this. These lapses were common and didn't mean Colleen loved her any less. But, oh, God, it hurt.

"Wait," Grace added. "If I could just use the restroom first?" She wanted to make sure there wasn't a curling iron still plugged in. And she needed a moment to splash some water on her face and collect herself.

When she came out of the bathroom, she found Colleen giggling at Ty, whose never-fail charm was once again working its magic.

Colleen brightened at the sight of her. "Gracie! I was just having the most delightful chat with... Oh, dear. What did you say your name was again?"

"Ty Beckett, ma'am." He met Grace's eyes, asking without words if she was all right, promising with his reassuring gaze that she would be. "I'm a friend of your daughter's."

"Then you're a lucky man," Colleen said impishly. "Because my Grace is a very special girl."

"Yes, ma'am. The most special I've ever known."

RATHER IMPOSSIBLY, GRACE had a good time at dinner. At least, as good a time as anyone could have when her heart was fractured; she wanted to strangle her oldest brother and she had a headache throbbing behind her left eye. Still, her brothers were on good behavior, and Maria was as entertaining as ever.

By the time they'd finished the meal and were taking their turns at the dessert buffet, she discovered that perhaps the reason for her brothers' subdued behavior wasn't her earlier threat. They both appeared preoccupied with women.

Ben caught up to her at the ice-cream dispenser, where she was making a slice of apple pie à la mode for Colleen.

He tugged on her sleeve. "Can I ask you a favor?" At her outraged are-you-freaking-kidding-me expression, he added defensively, "Hey, I've been nice to Beckett all night! I figured you'd want to reward me for that. Please, sis. It's important or I wouldn't have limped all the way over here to ask. It's a big room," he said, trying hard to look pathetic.

"If this dessert weren't for Mom, you'd be wearing it already. But I am curious about this favor."

"It's Amy. She won't talk to me. After you came by the booth yesterday, she got the whole story out of me, and she's furious. She accused me and Victor of being soulless cretins who are trying to destroy your happiness and put her out of a job. Then she… Never mind, that part's not important."

"Oh, no. If you're gonna ask for the favor, you have to tell me the whole story. Then she what?"

He scratched his chin. "She told me if I ever spoke to her again, she'd unman me with a swizzle stick."

Grace burst out laughing. *I love you, Ames.*

"I'm surprised she didn't tell you any of this," Ben said. "You two are so close."

Grace didn't think he needed to know she hadn't spent last night at home. "How did you and Victor *think* employees would react? That restaurant is important to a lot of people, not just me. You two treat me like running the place is some girlish indulgence, like believing in the tooth fairy, but I'm not a kid. I'm a businesswoman and a damn good chef."

"I know." He hung his head. "I never should have let Victor talk me into speaking with agents without you. Can I blame pain meds? He just seemed so convinced that selling the place would be best for you in the long run. He acted out of love, you know."

"Yeah, because that worked so well with Natalie," she muttered. Victor needed to stop trying to unilaterally protect the women in his life and try relating to them instead.

"What?" Ben asked.

"Nothing. One *tonto* brother at a time. Look, I'll talk to Amy, but I can't make any promises." She scanned his face. "This is important, huh?"

He looked away. "Of course. We all care about Amy. She's, you know, one of us."

Since he obviously wasn't ready to discuss his feelings—and the vanilla ice cream was melting—she returned to the table.

But she didn't have a chance to sit before Victor asked, "Can I talk to you? Out on the balcony? It's pretty tonight," he added lamely.

Exasperated, she glanced at Ty for moral support. He distinctly mouthed the words "only child" before stabbing into his key lime tart. *Lucky dog.*

She followed Victor out to the patio, where it was overcast and breezy. Her hair kept whipping into her face, and she had to hold it back with one hand just to see him. "Make it quick!"

"First, I'm sorry I hurt you by talking to the real-estate agents. I believe it was the prudent thing to do, so we can proceed quickly if we do go through with a sale, but I should have spoken to you first. Grace, he thinks he can get us a good deal. You could have practically the same life you do now, but with less pressure. You—"

"Stop! I didn't come outside to get this lecture again. You said 'first.' Maybe it would be best if you moved on to the second thing."

"Natalie." He closed his eyes, a pained expression tightening his face. "You said you spoke to her. How is she? Did she say anything about us? I…miss my wife."

She pinched the bridge of her nose. "Have you tried telling her that?"

"What would be the point? She threw me out."

"You're sure that's how it happened? Or did you think that was coming down the pike, so you bolted first?" The marital version of *you can't fire me, I quit.* "I know Natalie said some things she regrets. She's not blameless, but maybe you gave up too easily. Just like you want me to give up the Jalapeño," she added reprovingly.

"Selling something for a good price isn't the same as tucking your tail between your legs and running! I'm a realist, not a coward. If I talk Natalie into staying where she's unhappy, she'll either leave later or wish she had."

She shook her head sadly. "As long as you're manufacturing excuses not to try, I can't help you." She returned to the dining room, her skin chapped from the wind and her spirit equally abraded from everything that had happened today.

"I hate to rush you," she told Ty, "but are you ready to

go? I'm beat." She felt like a zombie. *Except I don't want brains, just a very soft mattress.*

They said their goodbyes—Colleen feeling comfortable enough to hug him timidly, Maria kissing him on both cheeks—and walked through the moonlit garden path back to her car. If the wind weren't swirling around in an angry howl, plastering her hair to her cheeks, it might have been somewhat romantic.

"Guess there's another storm blowing through," Ty commented.

His words soon proved true. The only noise in her car came from the fat raindrops that plunked against the roof and the rhythmic swish of windshield wipers. Ty neither asked about her talk with Victor nor commented on her mother's earlier confusion.

"You're quiet," she said.

"I didn't want to push. But I'm happy to listen."

She turned toward him. "Thank you. I appreciate that more than you can know. And I appreciate your being with me tonight."

"Well, neither of your brothers tried to drown me in my own soup, so I count dinner as a success."

When they got to his hotel, he said, "You know you're welcome to come in, right? You could stay the night or just wait out the rain."

"Another time?" she asked softly. "I wasn't kidding about being beat." She had planned to stop by the restaurant and see how things were doing, but she just wasn't sure she had it in her. Besides, the cook she'd left in charge would call her cell if anything was amiss.

Ty reached out to caress her cheek. "I'll see you tomorrow, then."

The chefs were each responsible for doing a cooking

demonstration at the *Road Trip* pavilion in the afternoon. Blessedly she could sleep in tomorrow morning.

"I planned to work the dinner shift tomorrow, but maybe Tuesday, we could work something out so that you could cook for me? Perhaps a really late dinner?" The benefit of owning the restaurant was she had access to it even when it was closed.

"Like I said, you name the time and place, and I'll be there. You want to help plan the menu, or can I surprise you?"

She laughed. "Since the day we met, Chef Beckett, you've done nothing *but* surprise me."

EVEN THOUGH AMY'S VEHICLE sat under the carport, when Grace let herself in the apartment, she discovered it empty. A note scrawled across the magnetic memo board on the fridge said Amy was at dinner with friends and Grace should text if she wanted Amy to bring her home dessert. Under the loopy scrawl of her signature, it read "P.S. Missed you last night," punctuated with a wicked smiley face. A second P.S. added "your brother is so on My List." Judging from the capital letters, it wasn't a good list.

Grace wondered if Amy had the same kind of budding feelings for Ben as he did for her. Her roommate had certainly never mentioned it. But maybe this was a new development, one Amy and Ben were only beginning to sort out themselves.

She made her way to the tiny closet they called a laundry room. It would help if she had clean clothes for the demo tomorrow—she wanted people to focus on the food, not the naked chef. As she sorted dark and light fabrics, she tossed around the idea of her brother and roommate together. Part of her was tickled at the possibility of two people she loved dating, but there could be complications. What would it be like in a few weeks, with Ty gone and Grace alone, sharing her apartment with a giggly couple in the early blush of new romance?

Maybe they can hang out at Ben's, and Victor can come over here to commiserate about how much we hate being single.

That was a weird thought. In the past, she'd valued her independence. She'd been more invested in the restaurant than in most of her dates. But now it was different. She was picturing her life with a Ty-shaped hole in it.

Would he think of her after he left? Would he miss her fondly or regret they'd become too involved? Grace found herself empathizing with Beth Beckett, the woman who had to wonder each day if her own son ever thought of her.

For a moment, unexpected anger scorched Grace. Did Ty even comprehend what he was throwing away so cavalierly? He'd said his mother got pregnant with him when she was a teenager, so the woman was relatively young. If they repaired their estranged relationship, they could still have years together. Decades! Didn't he know there were people in the world—people like Grace—who would give everything they had for another day with a loved one, for the chance to make a few more happy memories?

Done shoveling her clothes into the washer, she shut the door with a booming metallic clang. Ty wasn't going to be her future; she knew that. So if she did something, for his own good, that happened to anger him a little, would it matter? The worst he could do was never speak to her again, but that would probably happen over time anyway. She wanted to do something to make his life concretely better than it had been before he came here. How could she sit by and *not* help someone she… *Admit it, Gracie. You love him.*

She got her cell phone and dialed Information. A mechanical voice instructed her to say the city and state of the listing she needed.

"Roja, Texas."

Chapter Eleven

Dusk was falling Monday when Grace heard her name. Having completed a couple of separate instructional food demonstrations, she and Ty were headed to the parking lot and then his hotel. There had been talk of room service. And massages. It was with great reluctance that she turned to see who'd called.

Zane Winchester, Ben's Texas Ranger friend, strode toward her, his white hat and the star badge clipped to his belt identifying his job to others. A freckled brunette with wide cappuccino eyes was at his side; she was shaking like a leaf.

Since Zane didn't stop to explain who the woman was or exchange introductions with Ty, he was obviously on official business. "Grace, I understand you had a dessert demo a little while ago?"

She nodded, not sure why her churros were a matter for the Rangers. "Just finished up," she confirmed.

"And you gave samples to the crowd?" He held out a picture of a little girl with frizzy red curls and eyes that matched the woman's beside him. "This is Belle Hunt. Any chance you saw her? She has a sweet tooth, so I thought she might have gravitated toward a free dessert."

Grace's gut clenched in sympathy for Belle's mother. She took a hard look at the photo, willing herself to recognize the child. But after a minute she had to admit, "No, I'm sorry. Ty? Did you notice her?"

He shook his head. "Anything we can do to help with the search?"

"We already have police and over a dozen festival volunteers looking," Zane said. "We'll find her." He patted the brunette on the shoulder.

Even though Zane radiated confidence, Grace knew his words couldn't comfort the woman missing her baby.

Grace couldn't stand not to do anything. "Can I at least help check the women's restrooms? Maybe she just had to go potty and got lost."

"That would—" He held up a finger when a burst of static came out of his walkie-talkie. "Winchester here."

"This is Sandusky. We've got her, sir. Safe and sound."

Belle's mother began sobbing silently, her shoulders quaking as tears poured down her face in a deluge of relief and panic and sheer gratitude.

"Sandusky, put the little girl on so she can say hello," Zane commanded. "There's someone here who needs to hear her voice."

Misty-eyed, Grace edged away to give the emotional woman some privacy. "Can you imagine?" she asked Ty. "That poor mom. She must have been terrified. And Belle! The crowds here can be daunting for adults, let alone a lost child."

Ty gently squeezed the back of her neck. "It worked out all right."

"I know. Guess I've spent too much time with Donna. Now *I'm* crying over every little thing. But I can't imagine anything worse for a mother than not knowing if your child is okay. Wanting to hold them and being unable. Needing to see them with your own eyes and only having someone else's word for it that they're unharmed."

He rubbed his hand down her back as they navigated the parking lot. "Mrs. Hunt should be reunited with her daughter in the next five minutes. I'm sure she went through hell for however long they were apart, but she'll be fine as soon as she sees her kid."

About that. Grace gnawed at her lower lip. Dare she tell Ty what she'd done, the phone call she'd made? If all went according to plan, Beth Beckett's bus trip would get her here in time for Wednesday's cooking demonstration. The event was open to the public. Beth had just as much right to attend as a thousand other festivalgoers.

They got to Grace's car, but she made no move to unlock the doors. Instead she climbed up onto the hood. This wouldn't be easy, but he deserved to hear the truth. After all, wasn't that one of the reasons she'd been so furious with her brothers, because they'd gone behind her back? It wasn't too late to be honest with Ty. The terror-stricken part of her that wanted to throw up kept insisting she would lose him over this. *He was never yours to keep, anyway.*

"We need to talk," she admitted.

"Sounds serious. Is this about the competition?" He leaned on the front bumper. "If I had to lose to anyone, Grace, I'd want it to be you. I'm hoping that, however this works out, we can find it in ourselves to be happy for each other."

She gave him a sad smile. "A noble sentiment, but there are more important things in life than cooking competitions. Or even restaurants and cable deals. Do you know *why* the Jalapeño means so much to me?"

"Sure." He looked perplexed by her out-of-the-blue question.

"There are great quotes about how important our history is, about understanding your past and its connection to your future—not that I can think of an exact one right now." She studied the orange-and-red-streaked sky overhead as if the sunset might illuminate some answers, give her a better way to articulate what she wanted to express.

"I'm not following you, Grace. Are you trying to tell me you've built a time machine?"

"My heart about broke for that woman today," she said. "Just like my heart breaks for your mom. And for you."

He scowled, straightening abruptly. "You *have* spent too much time with Donna. Grace, try to understand, I don't have the background you do. I know it rips you up to be losing your mother, but Beth and I weren't close. She tried to fulfill her maternal obligation by not putting me up for adoption, but really, I'm not even sure that was for the best. I could have been with a nice foster home somewhere instead of that trailer—"

Fists clenched at his sides, he stopped. When he began speaking again, the telltale emotion was gone from his voice. "I'm not angry with her. I don't wish her ill. But even when we lived under the same roof, we barely had anything to talk about. Why pretend otherwise?"

"Because you have an opportunity other people don't!" She scrambled down off the car. "You can have a second chance. Maybe you won't become best buddies and start signing up for mother-son golf tournaments and cooking classes together, but you should at least face your past. Exorcise some demons, so they stop having so much power over you."

If he dealt with his past, would he be stable enough to share his future with someone? She brushed the thought away. She hadn't done this for her own gain; she'd done it for Ty.

He sighed, reaching for her. "If it's that important to you, I'll…send her a card at Easter."

A convenient offer for two months down the road, when Grace couldn't hold him to it. She squared her shoulders. Time to bite the bullet. "That, ah, won't actually be necessary. I called her for you."

"You what?" His voice was lethally soft. "Tell me you're kidding, Grace. As jokes go, this one sucks, but I'll forgive you if you say you're kidding."

She held his gaze although she wanted to flinch away from the raw, disbelieving fury in his steely eyes. "I got her number from Information, and I called her."

"And said what exactly? How did you even introduce yourself?" he thundered. "As my girlfriend? Because you would have sounded nuts if you told her you were some woman who's only known me a week and a half and has no business meddling in my life!"

"I told her the truth," she hollered back. "That I was someone who cares about you. A lot! And that you would be here the rest of the week if she wanted to come see you."

His face was mottled with anger. Thrusting a hand through his hair, he turned his back on her and strode away. Knowing how badly she'd shaken him, she let him go. Eventually he looped back in her direction.

"Call her again," he finally said. "Tell her you made a mistake."

"I don't think I did," she rebutted. "Ty, what's the worst that can happen? Let's say it's awkward and you decide after that the two of you don't want to speak for the next twenty years. How's that different from what you're already doing? You have nothing to lose."

"That's not your decision to make! You crossed a line, Grace." He glared. "I'm going to call Stephen or catch a ride to the hotel with one of the other chefs. You don't need to give me a lift—you've done more than enough."

FOR GRACE, TUESDAY AND Wednesday passed in a haze of misery and self-recrimination. She worked as many hours as she could at the Jalapeño, gave her public cooking demo on Wednesday with the vitality and enthusiasm of an automaton and let Amy nurse her through it all with frozen yogurt and pep talks.

"You did the right thing," Amy said from beneath her blanket on the futon Wednesday night.

Grace was curled up on the love seat. They'd decided to have a slumber party in the living room. The coffee table between them was littered with empty diet soda cans and junk food that hadn't nullified Grace's pain in the least.

"Maybe I *didn't* do the right thing," she said. "I arrogantly thought I knew best, like Victor. You know what they say about the road to hell being paved with good intentions." That's where she was now: hell.

On Tuesday, she hadn't seen Ty at all, which had cut since it was the day he was supposed to have cooked for her. She'd attended his presentation Wednesday afternoon, but she might as well have not been there. It wasn't that he'd coldly ignored her or turned away—he'd simply treated her as if she were another faceless stranger in the audience. If his megawatt smile happened to land on her, there was no special meaning in it, no sign in his gaze that he cared about her. Had his mother attended? Had he spoken to Beth or shunned her? Did the woman blame Grace for raising her hopes in vain?

Grace couldn't even ask Donna to spy for her. Yesterday morning, the blonde had experienced some sporadic contractions. She'd told Stephen that even though they were probably those phony Braxton Hicks contractions and not really the baby coming early, she'd feel better if she were at home, close to her obstetrician.

Donna had cried when she hugged Grace goodbye. "He'll come around!"

Stephen, who knew Ty better than anyone, had forced a smile but hadn't shared his wife's optimism. If Ty could walk away for so long from the woman who'd birthed him, why would he have any qualms about forgetting a woman he'd known such a short time, one he thought had betrayed his trust?

Grace smacked her fist into the sofa pillow. "I botched this good."

Amy licked the neon-orange cheese curl powder off her fingers. "You acted out of love. If he can't see that, he doesn't deserve you. I would hope that if it were me, for instance, you would interfere and help get me on the right path. You said he has practically no family? Then he needs her even more than most people need their moms. Which is considerable."

"He doesn't *want* to need anyone. I think the only reason he lets himself depend on Stephen is that he's on salary."

"Grace, you're entitled to grieve. He made you laugh and he was lovely to look at, but what you're describing is someone emotionally stunted. If he really can't let anyone in, the two of you would have detonated eventually with or without your sudden whim to play family therapist."

"You're right." But she felt no better. "I should call Ben and Victor, tell them I forgive them for knifing me in the back. They thought they were acting out of love, too."

Amy scowled, her philosophical mien vanishing. "I wouldn't be in any hurry to forgive those yahoos! You may get a cut of the sales price, but plenty of the rest of us won't. I know I could always move back to Austin, but I like it here!"

"We'll figure out something," Grace promised. "Who

knows? I might actually win that prize money." Tomorrow morning, the last challenge would be announced. They had a day for planning and preparation and would serve the judges on Friday.

In two days, Grace would learn her fate. She just hoped the next forty-eight hours went a lot better than the last forty-eight.

TY HADN'T REALIZED HOW heavily he relied on Stephen until the man was out of reach. Right before Ty went downstairs for his van ride to the final challenge reveal, he reflexively pulled out his phone and started to dial. Then he remembered Donna was on bed rest to help prevent premature labor and he should only call Stephen in case of extreme emergency.

Couldn't the case be made that Grace Torres ripping out his heart constituted a medical emergency? He still couldn't wrap his head around what she'd done. Yes, she'd made it clear family was important to her. But he'd made it equally clear that his past was private, not something to be dragged under a microscope for examination.

Almost as surprising as the fact she'd called his mother was the fact that Beth had come! He'd glimpsed her in the sea of faces yesterday when he'd been cooking in front of a live audience and had temporarily lost his train of thought. He'd recovered so quickly that hopefully no one noticed. Still, he wasn't accustomed to screwing up and blamed Grace for his uncharacteristic mistake.

Beth hadn't approached him after the presentation, however. She'd melted into the crowd, exacerbating his confusion. Was that it? Had she gone back home? Was she biding her time, trying to figure out what to say? Would she confront him publicly, let people know she was his mother? Surely she wouldn't try to insinuate that she'd taught him any of his craft? Why had she sent back the money from his most recent check?

The phone in his hand buzzed, startling him. He eyed it cautiously. Had Grace gone so far over the line as to give Beth his cell number? He'd included his Dallas phone number years ago with a check, but it wasn't as if he were ever home.

"Hello?"

"Where are you?" Reed Lockhart demanded amiably. "Katharine and I are waiting at the van."

"On my way." Ty disconnected, pausing just a moment by the mirrored closet door. What did he see in his reflection—a scrawny kid with bleak prospects, or a master chef with the skills to win tomorrow and continue building his legendary reputation?

He pasted his trademark smile on his face. No one passing him in the hotel hallways would be able to guess his thoughts were in turmoil or that he'd tossed and turned last night because he missed Grace and wished she were in his arms. He missed so many things about her. Maybe she'd done him a favor. He had far more incentive now to get over her than he'd had at the beginning of the week.

This was a cleaner break.

In the passenger van, he made small talk with Katharine and Reed. He wanted to behave as if nothing had changed. "Guesses on what the last challenge is?" he asked them. "Personally I think they're putting us in large vats of grapes, and we'll have to stomp our own wine, à la *I Love Lucy*."

"I hope it doesn't involve desserts," Katharine said. "They're not my forte."

Reed shrugged. "It's none of our specialties, really. I liked Jo, but at least with her gone, we're pretty evenly matched. If she were here for another dessert challenge, she'd trounce us."

"Grace might have a leg up there, too," Katharine cautioned. "Her restaurant had two fairly kick-ass desserts on the menu."

Grace's name exploded in Ty's head, as if he'd just tripped over a conversational land mine.

Seeing her ten minutes later was even worse. But he forced himself to include her in the casual nod he gave Damien and the camera crew. Though his gaze barely stayed on her a second, he couldn't help noticing the slight purplish crescents under her eyes. She hadn't been sleeping, either.

Not my problem.

"Well, this is it," Damien said. "The last obstacle between one of you and the grand prize! We all know food is meaningful. It can represent entire cultures, personal milestones, even how we feel about someone."

Ty's temples were pounding, and he wished he'd taken some aspirin. Damien's lengthy intro reminded him that he'd never had his chance to cook for Grace. *Her fault, not mine.* What would he have chosen for her? He'd been toying with ideas, but none had seemed quite right. They'd either been more pretentious than genuine, or they hadn't seemed good enough—a feeling Ty hadn't had about his food since his teens.

"For your final challenge," Damien said, "we're asking you to make the judges a very personal three-course meal. Choose any three dishes that somehow represent your past, your present and your future."

Now Ty *really* needed an aspirin. If it had been a week and a half later, he would have thought Grace put the host up to a lousy April's Fool joke at Ty's expense. What the hell was people's preoccupation with the past? And how could he represent his through food? It was the gas station challenge all over again, except he refused to stoop to that. He'd come up with something—seafood, maybe, because he'd lived close to the Gulf.

You can do this, Beckett. As long as the food he set in front of them was delectable, the judges weren't going to care about the explanation he formulated.

As for his "present" dish, would it be too on the nose to serve something inspired by Frederick-Fest? He could riff off of any number of German or Tex-Mex foods, but maybe he should think more broadly than that. And for the future…

His gaze skittered sideways, but he caught himself, bowing his head before he made eye contact with Grace. Whatever his future was, it wouldn't be here. And it wasn't with her.

"DON'T LOOK NOW," REED Lockhart said Thursday night, squinting in the dimness of the hotel bar, "but that woman is staring at you."

Ty didn't care. He was no more interested in women than he was in his untouched drink. But accepting Reed's friendly invitation had seemed better than returning to his room to mope about Grace. Thinking of her caused such a painful stab that he followed Reed's glance, desperate for any distraction. His fingers spasmed around his whiskey sour.

What in the hell was Beth doing there, standing off to the side?

Their eyes met. He couldn't pretend he hadn't seen her. He rose suddenly, not wanting her to disappear as she had Wednesday, leaving only unanswered questions behind. "That's…a relative," he told Reed. "I need to say hi."

"Sure thing. I should turn in after I finish this, anyway. Big day tomorrow!"

"The biggest," Ty agreed grimly.

He walked toward Beth, trying to read her expression in the low lighting. Up close, it was impossible not to see the joy in her eyes.

"Nathan," she breathed.

"Ty. Everyone calls me Ty. You look well," he said politely.

Though still slim, she'd rounded out since he last saw her. She'd always had a gaunt, pinched look. It occurred to him that *she* hadn't had any more to eat during his childhood than he had. He forgot that sometimes. Her clothes were worn, fraying at hems and pockets, and her light brown hair showed streaks of gray, but she looked better than he remembered. Her eyes and smile were like his, a resemblance he found disquieting.

"Why are you here, Beth?" The word *mom* stuck in his throat and refused to dislodge.

"I overheard this was where the cooking contestants were staying, and I worked up the nerve to come over. I was going to call your room and see if you would join me for a late dinner."

"I've eaten. But my question was more, why are you here in Fredericksburg? Why would a random phone call from a total stranger—one of my opponents, by the way—prompt you to hit the road? For all you know, this was some competitor's idea of a mind game."

Beth lowered her head, and he felt a twinge of guilt for taking out his frustration with Grace on his mother. But she rallied quickly. "I'll tell you why a random phone call caused me to jump on the next bus. Because it was the excuse I've been waiting for, the tiny sign I needed. Didn't Stephen tell you I... But he shouldn't have to tell my son that I want to see him. I should have written you directly, or called. It's been so long, though, I wasn't sure how. Sending back your money was a solid first step. Then when your girlfriend—"

"She's not."

"Your female friend. Nathan—Ty—I've been dying to see you ever since you left Roja." She turned toward the bar. "Can I get a drink? I think I need one."

"Sure. And we should get some food in you if you haven't had dinner." He hated to think of anyone being hungry. They sat at a nearby table and ordered a glass of wine and the appetizer sampler.

Beth smiled, looking drained but surprisingly content. "I'm so proud of you!"

You don't even know *me.* But he bit back the retort, recognizing he was as much to blame as Beth for their estrangement. He could have retraced his path home at any time.

"When you moved away, I figured it was for the best," she admitted. "I was young and stupid and didn't know much, but even I could see I stunk as a mother. Why hold you back?"

The gallant thing to do would be to assure her she hadn't stunk, but they both knew she hadn't been nurturing or maternal.

"It's not like I was a model son," he said woodenly.

"When you sent me that first check, I was touched. And, to be honest, I needed the cash. But over the years, I got more ashamed with each one I deposited. My child was doing more for me than I'd been able to do for you! It was galling. I tried to get better about saving up so there'd come a day I wouldn't need the money. I gave up cigarettes and hair dye, little things that added up after a while. I took extra odd jobs on weekends, like babysitting for another waitress I know. I'm not sure if it was the self-confidence from finally scratching together a few extra pennies or spending time with her little boy…but I got to thinking about you more and more. When Grace called, it was destiny. The time to see you had come."

"It wasn't destiny." *It was my interfering ex-lover who couldn't leave well enough alone.* "Look, I'm thrilled you're turning things around for yourself, but take the money. Please. I can afford it."

"I can't. Not if I'm ever going to respect myself."

The words struck an unexpected chord. In her way, Beth was seeking self-validation just like he was with the cable deal. They just had different measures of success. "Fair enough. I'll stop sending checks if you promise to call if you ever need anything."

"I need the years back. I wish I'd been a different mother to you."

He tried the cocky Ty Beckett smile. "Hey, I turned out *great*. No worries."

"Guess you can't be too bad if you have a girl like Grace in your life," she allowed. "Even in our short conversation, I could tell she's someone special."

Grace. He couldn't think about her, not with one day of cooking left and everything riding on tomorrow. "I hope this doesn't sound too rude, but I can't stay long. Tomorrow's the final day, and I need to rest." Not that going to his room would help him accomplish that—he'd learned that lesson from consecutive sleepless nights.

Beth nodded. "I have to catch a bus early, anyway. But I had to see you before I left. Maybe we'll talk again soon."

About what? he wondered. The twenty minutes he kept her company while she ate were painfully stilted. And he was Ty Beckett—the man who was supposed to be able to make small talk with anyone! But his mind went blank when he looked at her, disjointed scenes from his past rising in him like heartburn. He didn't dislike her, but he didn't have many nostalgic associations with her, either. He didn't breathe freely again until she stood to go.

"Good luck tomorrow," she said, hugging him awkwardly.

"Thanks." For the first time in his successful career, Ty was worried. The Beckett Instinct warned that he needed all the luck he could get.

BY NOON FRIDAY, GRACE HAD such a bad case of nerves that her stomach was in knots. She'd barely been able to taste-test her dishes because she was so queasy.

While Ty was out in the main dining room, taking his turn to present to the judges, Katharine came across the room. "You okay, hon? You look nervous. Don't forget you've done great in this competition!"

"Thanks." But great so far wasn't the same as ultimately winning. "I'm second-guessing my strategy, I suppose. It feels risky."

The door opened, and Ty walked in. He chose a spot next to Reed, but the stakes were higher today than they'd ever been and not even Ty was very chatty.

What seemed like a lifetime later, the production assistant opened the door and called Grace's name. Two waiters who'd been hired for the event helped transport her food to the dining room, where a panel of esteemed judges waited. The dishes from Ty's meal had already been cleared away, with no hint as to how much the judges had liked it.

"G-good afternoon," she greeted them. "I'm Grace Torres. The challenge today was to create something that represents our past, present and future. Personally I believe the three are inextricably linked, that sometimes they're shaped out of the same basic relationships and principles—the same ingredients, if you will, in different formations. To that end, I've created a three-course meal using cheese as my centerpiece. For your first course, I've adapted a fruit-and-cheese salad my mother used to make, topped with spices instead of dressing. The second course is a delicious cheese enchilada representing the restaurant my family owns and operates." *For now.*

Talking about her mom and the restaurant had caused her throat to go dry. In something of a croak, she added, "And your final course is a mini cheese soufflé. Um, enjoy." She scurried away from the table and their scrutiny. There had been more she'd wanted to explain about the soufflé, but it was too late now.

Her dishes would just have to sink or swim—and take her and the Jalapeño with them.

Hours passed before a final verdict was reached. The chefs had attempted to kill time by reading, playing game apps on their phones or, in Grace's case, pretending to sleep. She'd folded her arms on a tabletop and bowed her head, hoping to be left alone. If she and Ty had been the only ones in the room, she probably would have given in and apologized. Her guilt and curiosity were driving her nuts. Had he and his mother spoken? The additional audience of Katharine and Reed, however, made an already unpalatable discussion downright impossible.

Now, thank God, it was all over. For better or worse, the competition had ended. She could return to her life, and Ty would go.

"I just want to tell you," Damien began when the chefs stood in front of the judging table, "what a true honor this has been. You four are highly talented and represent some of the most exciting chefs to come out of Texas. It was an unbelievably difficult decision."

They started with Katharine, telling her she was a master chef and that it showed in every bite of her cuisine. However, they thought she'd largely rested on her laurels for this last challenge, without taking risks. Reed, on the other hand, had done nothing *but* take risks, with mixed results.

Make up your minds, Grace wanted to scream at the judges. The tension was getting to her.

They addressed her dishes next. "The presentation was a bit thin," one judge complained, "but the food itself was scrumptious."

A second judge made a face, shaking her head. "The salad was lovely, and the enchiladas were all right—but by the second course, it was feeling a bit heavy. So what did you finish us off with? A cheese soufflé! There should be more balance than that."

Grace's eye twitched. Damien had said that these courses should reflect the chef's life. Well, where was the balance in her world? For her first twenty-three years, she'd led a charmed existence. And for the past three? Problem after problem had mounted, and she was starting to doubt her capabilities to overcome them on her own.

You're not alone. You have Amy. And your brothers— when they aren't being buttheads.

She listened stoically to the rest of her critiques, wondering if they'd scored her or Katharine higher. Then they moved on to Ty.

The same judge who'd told Grace her presentation was "thin" called him on not having any real stories to go with his dishes. "Son, saying 'this is something I ate once a long time ago,' and 'this is something I ate more recently' is not representing your past, present and future. That said, this was some of the best food I've tasted in my entire life!"

The other judges echoed that opinion, and Grace knew the verdict before they formally announced it. Even still, hearing it out loud sent her world spinning. The floor gaped like a black jaw beneath her, waiting to swallow all her hopes and dreams.

"The winner," Damien boomed, "is Chef Ty Beckett!"

Chapter Twelve

"A deal's a deal," Grace said crisply. She and her brothers sat at Ben's kitchen table, the April sunshine glinting off the half-empty crystal pitcher of margaritas. "We'll sell."

Her brothers exchanged glances, not looking pleased or triumphant over her surrender.

"Is this because of...you-know-who?" Ben asked in hushed tones. "Amy thinks you're still hung up on him."

She tossed a wadded-up napkin at her brother. "Stop using me as an excuse to call my roommate and just ask her out."

Victor raised an eyebrow at that but stayed focused on topic. "If you need more time before we take this step—"

"You gave me two weeks already. Time won't make it easier. I'm burned-out." Which, in this case, was code for heartbroken. "An extended vacation might do me good. My only stipulation is that you find someone who will keep it alive as a restaurant—no bulldozing it to build a parking garage or something. And Rosie and Amy get the option of staying."

"That's all doable," Victor promised. "But what about you, Graciela? Don't you want the option of staying on as chef?"

She shook her head. "Maybe it is time to move on." That attitude had certainly served Ty Beckett well. She'd read in one of the articles that came out after his win that he'd been offered his own cable show. He'd gotten exactly what he wanted. Yippee for him.

But, as she kept trying to remind herself, she wasn't without blessings in her own life.

She reached across the table to squeeze Victor's hand. "I know I'm weepy, and this is a difficult thing we're doing. But when I was standing up for final judging in that competition, I thought about all the people in my life. You guys. Amy, Nat, Mom, Maria, half this town. I have just as many memories tied up in them as I do in the Jalapeño. At the end of the day, it's only a building. Maybe I was so upset because I'd…confused it for something more. I have to face reality. It's time to let go."

No matter how much it hurt.

"I THOUGHT YOU CALLING ME to sign these papers at the hospital was you being a workaholic," Ty joked. "Now I see it was just a clever ruse to get me to *ooh* and *aah* over the baby again."

"Like you need an excuse to fuss over her," Stephen retorted. "She's four days old, and you're already spoiling her rotten. You got her the biggest teddy bear in the state—and this is Texas, so that's saying something!"

"She's my goddaughter. It's my job." Ty smiled through the window of the preemie unit. "I know she's tiny, but she's already grown so much!"

"They're moving her into Donna's room as soon as a nurse is available. We should be able to go home in the next couple of days."

Ty clapped him on the shoulder. "I'm happy for you." He experienced a pang somewhere in his chest. He'd never really wanted the whole marriage-house-family package, but the Ziglers made it look really appealing, even after

Donna's early labor and difficult delivery. "You'll make great parents."

"Donna, especially," Stephen said as they walked toward the nearby coffee lounge, where Ty poured them each a cup. "Some women are natural-born mothers. They know they want kids and they have this way of relating to them… For other women, I guess it doesn't come so easily. Maybe they weren't expecting to get pregnant or got pregnant too young, but that doesn't mean they don't grow to love their children."

Ty grimaced. "That was the clunkiest segue I've ever heard in my life. If you want to ask about Beth, just do it."

"Well, since you brought her up… Have you talked to her since you left Fredericksburg?"

"Once." Which, admittedly, was more than he had in the past decade. "I called to tell her I won, and she congratulated me. But we don't know each other, Stephen."

"They have a cure for that—talking. The more you do, the more you'll learn about each other. I realize it's a pretty radical treatment, but it's covered by most insurance."

Ty rolled his eyes. "You've officially been cooped up in this hospital too long. Your metaphors are worse than ever."

Stephen slumped into a chair. "I need lessons from Grace on how to say things straight. I don't have her moxie."

Ty almost sloshed coffee down his front—after two and a half weeks, mention of Grace could still make him shaky. "I said you could ask about Beth," he clarified. "Grace is off-limits."

"Not yet, she isn't! If you say we can't talk about Grace, then after today, we won't. But first, you're gonna hear me out."

Ty narrowed his eyes. "Tread carefully. My darling goddaughter needs her father to stay employed."

Stephen made a rude noise. "In the past seven years, I've grown quite the client portfolio. I don't need you, Beckett. But I think Grace Torres does. Are you blind? You couldn't have missed the way she looked at you."

No, he wasn't blind. He still dreamed about the way she'd looked at him. The way she'd touched him, the way she'd listened, the way she'd made him laugh, the way she'd trusted him.

He resented Stephen painting him as the villain in this piece. "Grace and I were always temporary—that was the deal."

"And what do you have me do when we're offered a shoddy deal?" Stephen prompted. "We counteroffer, renegotiate! When you first met Grace, maybe you didn't know how special she was. Maybe it was supposed to be temporary. But in light of how good you two were together, how much she loved you—"

"She acted without any regard for my feelings!"

"At least she had enough faith in her conviction to tell you what she'd done. Like I said, I'm not as skilled at straight shooting." Stephen chugged a gulp of the truly horrible hospital coffee.

"Truth time," Stephen declared. "I've been sending your mom little updates about you for a long time. I looked for ways to instigate contact and hint that you'd like to hear from her without ever telling an outright lie. My way was the wussy way. Grace bypassed that and just picked up the phone, braving your wrath in order to give you a gift."

What, the gift of one awkward reunion dinner and a couple of strained phone calls? "I'm over thirty, Stephen. I don't need a mommy."

"You damn sure needed something. You were a bitter man, Ty, and eventually the bitterness was going to bleed through that charm you wield. At least Grace lifted up the dust ruffle so you could look under the bed and see that your past wasn't the bogeyman." Stephen made a face. "Okay, that was a truly terrible metaphor."

"It's probably the hospital coffee. This muck has to be destroying our brain cells." Which would explain why, for a minute there, everything Stephen said had made total sense.

"All right, enough with the unsolicited advice," Stephen promised. "I called you here to look over the final draft of the contract. You sign this, you officially become the host of your own prime-time television show." He handed over a manila envelope. "I've looked at it, the lawyer's looked at it. All that's left is for you to take a last look and decide once and for all…is this really what you want your future to be?"

THE CALL GRACE HAD BEEN dreading came on a Tuesday night. When she'd told Victor to find a seller, she hadn't realized he would do it so quickly. But then, that's exactly what he'd said he'd do, the reason he'd taken care of preliminary inspections and appraisals and had so many meetings with the real-estate agent. Victor was thorough and efficient.

Truthfully he could handle the entire closing without her, but he was making a concerted effort to treat her like an equal partner and not his kid sister. Besides, sticking her head in the sand and letting her brothers take care of everything was the coward's way out. Her father wouldn't have approved.

"Can you meet us there at ten in the morning?" Victor asked. "All involved parties can discuss the conditions of sale. I swear, Grace, if you're not satisfied by the offer, we won't take it. But I honestly believe this proposal has the best terms we're going to find."

"I trust you," she assured him. "And I'll see you in the morning."

She woke up far too early the next day and couldn't go back to sleep, so she occupied her time by making a huge breakfast for Amy—pancakes, eggs, fruit. Grace took one bite, and her stomach roiled, so she left the table to get dressed. She chose all black—a slim-fitting knee-length skirt that hugged her hips, and a black-on-black checked blouse. All the jewelry she picked had been handed down by her mother; she wanted to feel close to her parents today.

After redoing her eye makeup twice and cleaning all the breakfast dishes, there was nothing left to do but face the inevitable.

Even though she was a couple of minutes early, she was surprised not to see Victor's car in the lot. Then again, maybe that sedan she didn't recognize belonged to his agent. They probably rode together. Her power heels (the highest she owned, putting her at five-four) crunched across the gravel, and even though she knew it was only in her head, when she opened the back door, she imagined she heard one of those ominous horror-movie creaks.

Get a grip, Gracie. You're not going to meet your doom. Try to look at it as meeting your future. She'd grown up assuming her career choices had already been made. Now she'd be free to reexamine them, maybe make some changes. It would be a character-freaking-building experience.

"Hello?" she called. "Vic?"

"He's not actually coming." A man in a white button-down shirt and dark slacks stepped out of her office, giving her a smile so shy that for a moment she was confused about his identity. Did Ty Beckett have an identical twin? Because this man looked just like Ty, except for his bashful air.

She tried to suck in enough oxygen to make her brain function. "You can't be here! You won. The unspoken deal was that you'd get the hell out of my town and leave me to nurse my wounds."

"It was a lousy deal, Grace." He took a step toward her. There was the Ty she remembered—the self-assured man who got his way because he was able to convince other people it was what they wanted. "I'd like to renegotiate."

"Do my brothers know you're here, or did you trick them somehow?"

"Oh, they know. They each interrogated me at length about my intentions before they agreed to this."

"Your intentions?" Her heart fluttered.

"This will be easier to explain in the dining room." He held out his hand. "Will you come with me?"

Her mind was still screaming. *Why* was he here? Should she be happy to see him? Should she play the aloof former lover, tell him it had been nice while it lasted but that his hanging on like this was embarrassing? *Good luck pulling that off.* Aloof wasn't really in her repertoire. Part of her wanted to hit him over the head with her purse; the other part wanted to drag him back into the office and cover him with kisses.

She followed him but declined to take his hand.

"I worried you'd come through the front, which would ruin the surprise, but Vic said you usually use the back door."

She blinked. It was quite a surprise indeed. Rose petals of all different colors were strewn across booths and tabletops. Candles had been placed throughout the dining room, and overhead, an Irish Tenors CD her mother loved played softly.

"I don't understand," she said. "This looks like a…" *Seduction.* "An apology."

"I never got to cook for you," he said. "It's one of the many things I've regretted. And I was hoping to make it up to you. Will you have a seat? I'll be right back. Just please don't leave before you've heard me out."

There was something so boyishly eager and unsure about his tone. It stunned her that Ty was unsure about anything; it flattered her beyond belief that the uncertainty was over *her.* True to his word, he returned in a flash. He carried a tray with three plates on it and set the tray on a table behind him, so she couldn't get a good look at the food.

"Grace, you've tried to get me to talk about my past, to accept it, and the truth is, I was scared. But you make me brave. Since meeting you, since falling for you…"

Tears pricked her eyes. She couldn't believe this was happening. And she couldn't believe her brothers had conned her!

"I have three plates here. They represent my past, present and future." With a flourish, he set the first plate in front of her. A lump of unappetizing hamlike substance sat surrounded by soda crackers.

"Well." She sat back in her chair. "That's not what I expected."

"Just between you and me," he whispered loudly, "I wouldn't eat it. Stuff is vile. But it's my past. I'm learning to be okay with that. Here, let me get that out of your way."

He replaced the first plate with a second one, larger and fancier. "This represents my present. Grilled skirt steak with chimichurri two ways and a side of grilled asparagus with farm fresh eggs and olives, topped with shaved cheese. It was the exact meal I cooked for the pilot episode of my show. Which, I regret to inform you, will not be airing."

She jerked around in her chair. "What? Did they change their minds?"

"No." He held her gaze. "I did. Which brings us to plate number three, my possible future." He handed her a plate with a lengthy document on it.

"I'm not eating the papers," she told him. "I don't care what you seasoned them with."

"Definitely don't eat them," he agreed, sliding into the seat next to her. "This is a partnership document Stephen drew up for me. For you *and* me, for the Jalapeño."

"What?" This wasn't all just an elaborate way to get her to listen, he actually was the buyer Victor had found?

"I know it's presumptuous. This is a family restaurant, and you and I aren't family…yet. But we could buy out your brothers and make this place as great as it deserves to be. I've thought a lot about what you said, Grace, and I want to build something real and lasting. I want to put down roots and let people into my life." He leaned close enough to thread his hands through her hair. His breath brushed over her face, sending tingles of awareness through her. "One person in particular. If she'll have me."

If she'd have him? She couldn't imagine any more miserable weeks like the ones without him. Grace threw her arms around him. "I love you. *Te amo,* Nathan Tyler Beckett."

He kissed her passionately, his tongue delving into her mouth, his hands stroking along her body saying all the things he hadn't yet put into words. Grace shook with need. She'd missed him so much that it didn't take more than a few minutes of kissing to melt her.

She pulled back slightly. "The restaurant doesn't open for lunch for two more hours, and the office door locks."

He shot to his feet. "Lead the way."

As they hurried down the hallway, she gave him a saucy smile over her shoulder. "Does this mean you aren't mad at me anymore?"

"Only mad *about* you, sweetheart."

Epilogue

The night before the grand reopening of The Twisted Jalapeño in May, there was a private reception for select friends and family. It was one of the happiest evenings of Grace's life. Her brothers were there, naturally, and both brought dates. As she'd once feared, Amy and Ben were obnoxiously sappy and always together at the apartment—so it was just as well that she spent most of her time at Ty's new place. Victor and Natalie were also together; they'd been dating for a couple of weeks and had survived their first counseling session.

"It was difficult," Natalie had confided. "Really painful, but, as long as this works, really worth it."

If the smiles on their faces were any measure, Grace thought they just might make it.

Her aunt was in attendance, as well as Beth Beckett. Ty thought it was time his mother and fiancée officially met—the two had talked on the phone several times and Ty had admitted that all of Grace's talk about the wedding plans was helping him bridge the gap. At least he had something specific and upbeat to discuss with his mom whenever conversation stalled. Donna and Stephen came with their adorable bundle of joy, the tiniest, most perfect baby girl Grace had ever seen.

"I can't believe you named her Tyler anyway!" she'd

cackled when she heard the news. But she had to admit that Tyler McKenzie Zigler had a nice ring, and Ty didn't seem to mind sharing his name with a six-pound infant clad in head-to-toe pink.

Grace firmly shot him down when Ty suggested they retaliate by naming their first daughter Stephen.

The guest of honor at the reception was Colleen, who spent the entire night with a dreamy smile on her face. "You two have done such a lovely job with the place. It looks exactly like it did when your father was alive."

Biting her lip, Grace glanced around. It looked *nothing* like that. But it felt the same—like home and love and great food and special memories.

Grace hugged her mother. "I love you, Mom."

Colleen squeezed her back. "You, too, Gracie. And here's your handsome young man," she said when Ty joined them.

Although Colleen hadn't been able to help plan any of the wedding details, she seemed to enjoy hearing about them. So Ty and Grace kept her entertained with a list of their decisions so far.

"It's all coming together," Ty said proudly. "Except of course for the catering fiasco."

Grace looked at him blankly. "What fiasco?"

He winked at her. "Turns out, the two best chefs in Texas are already busy that day."

* * * * *

HEART & HOME

COMING NEXT MONTH
AVAILABLE MAY 8, 2012

#1401 A CALLAHAN WEDDING
Callahan Cowboys
Tina Leonard

#1402 LASSOING THE DEPUTY
Forever, Texas
Marie Ferrarella

#1403 THE COWBOY SHERIFF
The Teagues of Texas
Trish Milburn

#1404 THE MAVERICK RETURNS
Fatherhood
Roz Denny Fox

HARCNM0412

REQUEST YOUR FREE BOOKS!

2 FREE NOVELS PLUS 2 FREE GIFTS!

LOVE, HOME & HAPPINESS

YES! Please send me 2 FREE Harlequin® American Romance® novels and my 2 FREE gifts (gifts are worth about $10). After receiving them, if I don't wish to receive any more books, I can return the shipping statement marked "cancel." If I don't cancel, I will receive 4 brand-new novels every month and be billed just $4.49 per book in the U.S. or $5.24 per book in Canada. That's a saving of at least 14% off the cover price! It's quite a bargain! Shipping and handling is just 50¢ per book in the U.S. and 75¢ per book in Canada.* I understand that accepting the 2 free books and gifts places me under no obligation to buy anything. I can always return a shipment and cancel at any time. Even if I never buy another book, the two free books and gifts are mine to keep forever.

154/354 HDN FEP2

Name   (PLEASE PRINT)

Address   Apt. #

City   State/Prov.   Zip/Postal Code

Signature (if under 18, a parent or guardian must sign)

Mail to the **Reader Service:**
IN U.S.A.: P.O. Box 1867, Buffalo, NY 14240-1867
IN CANADA: P.O. Box 609, Fort Erie, Ontario L2A 5X3

Not valid for current subscribers to Harlequin American Romance books.

Want to try two free books from another line?
Call 1-800-873-8635 or visit www.ReaderService.com.

* Terms and prices subject to change without notice. Prices do not include applicable taxes. Sales tax applicable in N.Y. Canadian residents will be charged applicable taxes. Offer not valid in Quebec. This offer is limited to one order per household. All orders subject to credit approval. Credit or debit balances in a customer's account(s) may be offset by any other outstanding balance owed by or to the customer. Please allow 4 to 6 weeks for delivery. Offer available while quantities last.

Your Privacy—The Reader Service is committed to protecting your privacy. Our Privacy Policy is available online at www.ReaderService.com or upon request from the Reader Service.

We make a portion of our mailing list available to reputable third parties that offer products we believe may interest you. If you prefer that we not exchange your name with third parties, or if you wish to clarify or modify your communication preferences, please visit us at www.ReaderService.com/consumerschoice or write to us at Reader Service Preference Service, P.O. Box 9062, Buffalo, NY 14269. Include your complete name and address.

The heartwarming conclusion of

from fan-favorite author
TINA LEONARD

With five brothers married, Jonas Callahan is under no
pressure to tie the knot. But when Sabrina McKinley
admits her bouncing baby boy is his, Jonas does
everything he can to win over the woman he's loved
for years. First the last Callahan bachelor must uncover
an important family secret…before he can take
the lovely Sabrina down the aisle!

A Callahan Wedding

**Available this May
wherever books are sold.**

www.Harlequin.com

HAR75405

*After a bad decision—or two—Annie Mendes
is determined to succeed as a P.I. But her first assignment
could be her last, because one thing is clear: she's not cut
out to be a nanny. And Louisiana detective Nate Dufrene
seems to know there's more to her than meets the eye!*

*Read on for an exciting excerpt of the upcoming book
WATERS RUN DEEP by Liz Talley...*

THE SOUND OF A CAR behind her had Annie scooting off the
road and checking over her shoulder.

Nate Dufrene.

Her heart took on a galloping rhythm that had nothing to
do with exercise.

He slowed beside her. "Wanna ride?"

"I'm almost there. Besides, I wouldn't want to get your
seat sweaty."

His gaze traveled down her body before meeting her
eyes. Awareness ignited in her blood. "I don't mind."

Her mind screamed, *get your butt back to the house and
leave Nate alone.* Her libido, however, told her to take the
candy he offered and climb into his car like a naughty little
girl. Damn, it was hard to ignore candy like him.

"If you don't mind." She pulled open the door and
climbed inside.

The slight scent of citrus cologne, which suited him,
filled the car. She inhaled, sucking in cool air and Nate.
Both were good.

"You run often?" he asked.

"Three or four times a week."

"Oh, yeah? Maybe we can go for a run together."

Her body tightened unwillingly as thoughts of other
things they could do together flitted through her mind. She

shrugged as though his presence wasn't affecting her. Which it *so* was. Lord, what was wrong with her? *He* wasn't her assignment.

"Sure." No way—not if she wanted to keep her job. As he parked, she reached for the door handle, but his hand on her arm stopped her. His touch was warm, even on her heated flesh.

"What did you say you were before becoming a nanny?"

Alarm choked out the weird sexual energy that had been humming in her for the past few minutes. Maybe meeting him on the road wasn't as coincidental as it first seemed. "A real-estate agent."

Will Nate discover Annie's secret?
Find out in WATERS RUN DEEP by Liz Talley,
available May 2012 from Harlequin® Superromance®.

And be sure to look for the other two books
in Liz's THE BOYS OF BAYOU BRIDGE series,
available in July and September 2012.

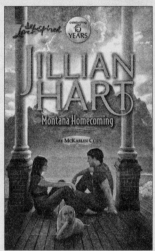